THE SWORD OF
JUSTICE

J. ALSPAUGH

DEDICATION

This book is dedicated to the true King of kings in gratitude for His righteous rule and tender mercies.

"For the word of the Lord is right, and all His work is done in truth. He loves righteousness and justice; The earth is full of the goodness of the Lord."

Psalm 33:4-5

CHAPTER 1

"Justice, I wish you would not come here." The graying man set a plate of food in front of Justice, leaning in confidentially as he spoke. "It makes my customers nervous." He glanced around the run down tavern and smiled weakly at those who were watching.

"Then perhaps you should be more choosey about who you let into this fine establishment, Dorian," Justice responded, picking up his fork. He examined it, wiping it clean with his thumb. "If I am here for any of them, I will let them know when the time is right."

Dorian wrung his hands uncomfortably. His tavern was his life. All around him, men sat at sturdy, wooden tables and chairs scarred by years of use. Usually, they laughed and talked loudly as they ate, filling the room with the raucous sound. Today, however, was different. Dorian's customers spoke in low tones, their posture secretive and unwelcoming. They were all aware that it was a King's Man who sat among them. Though he was average in height and appearance, there was a commanding air about him that set Justice apart from the others. Toned and wary, he paid them no mind as they glanced hatefully at him. Many had never seen Justice before, but his name and reputation were known by all. There was not a man living who dared to cross blades with Justice without a cause.

A thin man with a wiry mustache scurried over to where

Justice sat. "You let Old Joe finish his steak and head home before you killed him." The man's appearance and movements were disturbingly like those of the rats that moved in the shadows of the tables looking for scraps.

Justice cut into his steak, ignoring the rat-like intruder.

"Who's it to be this time, Justice?" He rasped in a loud whisper, "Who are you here to kill?"

The room fell silent, waiting for his answer. They waited in vain. Justice went on eating as if he were alone.

"It's one of us, isn't it?" a big man asked, getting to his feet. "I'm not going down without a fight. You murderous assassin." The big man stood there intimidating those around him but having no effect on the assassin he sought to impress. After an awkward silence, broken only by the light clink of Justice's knife and fork, the big man huffed and stormed out of the room.

A few drunks guffawed at the failed challenge and the cat calls began.

"Not up to a fight, are we?" a burly man bellowed. "Has your reputation outgrown you?"

"Are you here for my Mum?" a drunk asked staggering towards where Justice sat. His friends grabbed him and drug him back to his place. He laughed and told the others in a loud, confidential whisper, "She's knocked off a few men in her time."

"Look at him, as deaf as a fencepost. Maybe that's why he finds killing so easy."

"He's not human, has no heart. How else could a man go around killing his fellow men?" The last comment was from Dorian's wife. Justice had killed her brother two years ago, and she was determined never to forget. If she had her way, she would have poisoned him long ago, but Dorian would not permit it. Justice was a King's Man. A man who had sworn allegiance to the king and who was backed in power by the full authority of the king himself. Though Justice rarely summoned them, he himself had the authority to enlist the help of the king's soldiers whenever it was needed. And so, because Dorian feared the king's army, Justice ate only the best at his tavern. The questions and threats continued unheeded by the assassin. He ate, wiped his mouth, and rose from the table. From a small leather pouch on his belt, he removed a single coin which he placed on the table beside his plate. For the first time since he entered the tavern, Justice looked slowly around the room. Meeting each glaring face with an unnerving calm. A few men rose and left quickly. Justice knew by their defiant looks that he would return for them someday. Others crept out in fear, guilt driving them to hide from his steady gaze. Satisfied that his man was not in the room, Justice left without a word. He was there to kill, and he had never missed his man.

CHAPTER 2

"Oh no." She backed away from the door clutching her apron to her heart. She was young and pretty, but Justice could see the marks of hardship in her expression. Her soft red hair was pulled back from her face and rested in waves on her shoulders. With his sword drawn, Justice entered the house. The furniture was scarce, only the necessities. A worn blanket hung from the ceiling concealing a makeshift room in one corner.

Unable to speak, she backed away. Her green eyes moving fearfully to the older man who sat in an arm chair by the fire. At first glance, he could have been anyone's grandfather. He sat with a quilt across his knees, his loose flannel shirt spoke of the muscular man he had been in the past. Sickness had robbed him of his heath and now, thin and stooped, he sat minding the fire.

"Wiley Oliver, the king has sent me." Justice's strong voice filled the room.

The old man started and turned toward the door. His eyes were hard and cold. "What business does the king have with me?" he demanded, still holding the poker in the flames of the low fire.

"Your time has come."

"But why are you killing him?" The young lady had found her voice and went to stand beside Wiley. "What has he done?"

Reaching inside the leather pouch at his side, Justice pulled out an official letter, sealed with the king's seal. Breaking the seal, Justice opened the letter and read it aloud. "By order of the king, Wiley Oliver has been found guilty of the cruel murder of Counselor Hillcrest and his wife. This dastardly deed was confirmed by clear evidence and numerous eye witnesses before the throne of judgment. By order of the king, and the king's court, Wiley Oliver is hereby sentenced to die. No substitution will be accepted." Justice met the man's hard eyes before going on. "The sentence is to be carried out by Justice Spear at once. Signed with the king's own hand, etc." Justice finished as he folded the letter and placed it back into his pouch.

The girl covered her mouth with both hands as if the thought were too much to bear. "But why must he die? Can you show no mercy?" she begged.

Justice looked at her with a confused frown. She was at least 16 years old, perhaps barely 18. Old enough to understand the clear verdict from the king. "I just read you the reason." He pointed at the leather pouch at his side as if to remind her.

"But is there no other way? No mercy at the throne of the king?" She fell dramatically on her knees.

"For a murderer?"

"You are a murderer!" She shot back, emotions flaring.

"No, I am an assassin." Justice looked at her once more, fascinated by her simple mind. "I bring the king's sentence to those who have earned death." Moving his attention past the kneeling girl, Justice met the hard eyes of Wiley Oliver. "Wiley Oliver, did you kill Counselor Hillcrest and Lady Hillcrest?"

A little sound escaped the girl, but Justice kept his eyes on the old man.

"I did." The man sneered, his poker was glowing hot

now and Justice knew he planned to use it as a last resort to escape death.

"By your own admission, and the order of the king, your sentence is death." Justice's voice was steady and clear. He hesitated with a glance at the girl who was getting up and brushing off her skirts. "Do you want me to do it with her here?" he gestured at her with his thumb.

"Anna Lea, go to your room. I have business with this man." His glare silenced her protest, and she hurried through a curtain into a back part of the house.

She heard a metallic clash. A moment later, something heavy fell to the wooden floor. There was a scraping sound, the door creaked, and the house fell silent.

The silence stretched on until she called tentatively, "Pa?"

"It is done." Justice answered heavily. "Do you want me to help you bury him?"

She came out slowly, her eyes wide with fear. Glancing around the room she looked at him questioningly.

"The body is outside." Justice informed her. He had been cleaning his sword and tossed the rag into the fire. The poker lay unused on the floor, its fading red tip burning a harsh black groove in the floorboard where it rested.

"The body? My pa you mean!" she hurried past him into the yard. The quilt that had been resting on the old man's knees only minutes before, now covered the body of the killer. She knelt beside it, not daring to touch even the blanket that hid him.

Justice sheathed his sword and followed her. "He is not your father."

She looked up at him, shocked.

Following him to the shed beside the house, she demanded an explanation.

"If he were your father," Justice responded, poking around among the tools in the dim shed. "You would have had some

emotion towards him. You had wooden pleas but no tears."
Justice located a shovel and made his way back to the body.
"He was unkind to you. When he sent you from the room,
his look alone caused you to tremble."

Holding her head high, she met his brown eyes with her
own fierce glare. "And now what? I have no provision, no
way to live. You have killed him quickly, but my death will
be slow and painful."

"The king in his mercy has made provisions for the
widows and such."

"I suppose I am 'and such' to you." Anna Lea snapped.

Justice shrugged, "Be whatever you want to be. It makes
no difference to me." He looked around the bare yard and
chose a place where the shaded dirt would be soft yet far
enough from the tree to avoid roots.

"I am sorry," she said it softly, and he did not hear it
over the sound of the shovel cutting through the earth. She
fidgeted with the edge of her apron for a moment before
trying again. "I said I was sorry."

"For what?" he asked, sparing her a glance before driving
the shovel in once more.

"Shouting and such." Anna Lea was irritated by the absent 'oh' he gave in response. "What were you saying about
a place I could go?"

"The king has places of refuge scattered across the realm.
Those who are bereaved or in need can flee there for protection. There they will teach you a trade with which you
may earn your livelihood. Housing is provided as long as
the work is satisfactory. The nearest refuge is the Weaver's
Refuge. Many of the widows I encounter go there."

"You mean the widows you create."

Justice shrugged in response. Pacing off the length of
the shallow ditch he had made, he glanced over at the body.
The calculations done, he removed his sword and placed it

against the tree a few yards away. Stepping into the ditch he started to dig once more. The hole was to size now and only needed to be deepened.

"Do you bury all your victims?" Anna Lea asked crossing her arms.

"No."

"Why bury my Pa?"

The hole was deepening fast. She could tell he had done this many times before. "He's not your pa" Justice reminded her.

She pursed her lips. "Then why bury Wiley Oliver?"

He glanced up at her, amused. "So you will have time to grieve by the body."

Putting her hands on her hips, she glared at him again. "Well, I'm not grieving. He was a cruel man." She caught herself and added, "At least I had a place to stay and food to eat. That's more than you can offer."

"I'm not offering anything beyond this grave," Justice corrected her. "The king offers housing and work. Not me."

"Very well, I will travel with you and help you."

Anna Lea was startled by the hard, cold look the assassin gave her. Up to this point, he had acted like a gentleman, no hate, no malice, just doing his job. Now, his face showed emotions that made her uncomfortable.

"You think this is a game? A simple task, like planting a garden that you can help with?" He demanded, eyes blazing. "You think it is easy to walk up to a man and end his life, leaving his family to fend for themselves? Do you actually think I enjoy what I do?" He glared at her until she looked away. "You find yourself another life and leave me out of it." He turned back to his digging.

"I could make you something to eat, something to take with you," she offered softly.

"Go pack your things. It is several day's ride to the Weaver's Refuge."

"Oh good, I was afraid I would have to go alone." He stopped and looked up at her with the same confused frown she had seen when she asked if he would spare Wiley Oliver.

"You are going alone." Justice said the words slowly to insure she caught each one. "Not with me, not with my horse, not with him," he gestured to the dead man. "You will be alone. You will want to pack food and travel in the day time, because you will be traveling alone. By yourself."

"I'm not a simpleton," she answered, storming off toward the house.

"I would bet some money on that if I were a betting man," Justice muttered digging faster. The sooner he was away from her the better.

"So it was poor Wiley Oliver." The rat-like voice came from above.

The hole was a little over four feet deep now, and Justice was painfully aware that his blade stood useless out of reach. He dug on as if he had not heard, weighing his options. It was he who was the simpleton now.

"You have it that deep, you might as well finish it up and lay down in it." Another voice boomed.

Justice recognized it as the big man from the bar. He stopped digging and looked up. The rat-like man and the big man were not alone. Three or four others stood around. One held Justice's sword.

"What is it you want?" Justice asked. There was no way to gracefully climb out of a half dug grave. By their faces he knew they would not allow him out if he tried.

The men grinned at one another. "We want to be rid of you."

"My business here is done." Justice answered, looking into the face of each of the men. Only one, the youngest, showed the slightest hint of mercy. "I can leave now if you prefer."

"He's so accommodating now that he does not have his sword." The big man was still sore about being ignored in the tavern. The others laughed.

"Thanks for the new sword, Justice. It will look real nice…"

The big man snatched the sword from the speaker. "Are you out of your mind? You can't keep it. If the king's soldiers find it at your house, they will kill you."

"I didn't think of that, Milo." He wiped his hands off as if the king's soldiers would be able to see he had held it.

"No, you didn't," Milo mocked. "You hold it, Rats." Shoving the sword into the thin man's hand, Milo walked closer to the hole. "Lay down in it."

Justice looked up at Milo and knew he had no choice. He was outnumbered and in a hole which were two deadly disadvantages. Milo grabbed the top of the shovel and jerked it from Justice's hand. "Lay." He commanded.

Getting down on his stomach. With his elbows by his sides, Justice put his hands under his face, digging a little extra space for air in the soft dirt. The first shovelful of dirt hit the back of his head. Justice forced himself to stay calm. There would be only one way to get out of this, and he would have to keep his wits about him if he wanted to pull it off. Dirt rained down on his back and legs. Justice waited, biding his time. As the dirt thickened on his back, Justice moved his hands slowly downward toward his shoulders making sure his elbows did not push up through the dirt. Again, he waited. Above he could hear the jeering voices. Several of the men were drunk. They would not remember what they had done in the morning. Another layer was added, and Justice pressed against the dirt raising his body slightly and giving himself more air to work with in the empty space his chest had occupied. It was a mental test, and a test of strength as Justice inched his upper body upward. If he moved too fast, they would see the movement or the difference in the way the dirt lay. He had to raise himself onto his hands and knees if he hoped to withstand the weight of the dirt that would rest on him. His movements were slow and calculated as he pushed himself up against the ever increasing weight of the dirt on his back. Their voices were muffled by the layer of dirt. Though the light no longer reached him, Justice kept his eyes open. He braced himself, his arms fully extended. Pulling his legs forward one at a time, he worked himself to a crawling position and was still, waiting silently beneath the earth. The small chasm he had created held all the air he could access. He waited, braced. Someone stepped onto the dirt above and walked about, packing the thick layer of dirt. Justice held against the extra weight, doing his best to protect the pocket of air beneath him. Again he waited, keeping his breathing even. If there was anything Justice hated, it was small spaces. There was another impact, but he was ready for it. He could hear very little now, yet he waited, tense and ready.

Without warning, a shining metal shaft sliced Justice's face and embedded itself in the dirt between the fingers of his right hand. He gasped, forcing himself not to move. It was the blade of his sword. A few inches in any direction would have cost him his escape. He could feel blood oozing from the cut on his temple and cheek. It was not deep. He tried not to think about what could have happened. Fear gripped him. Justice, the king's assassin, feared by all, now found himself sweating and choked by fear. If they drove his sword in again? Justice did not dare to think of it. He waited, sweat and blood mingling in a stinging line down his face. If he moved early, it could cost him his life. But if he waited too long, the outcome would be the same.

CHAPTER 3

Justice waited for what seemed like an eternity. Finally, when he could stand it no longer, he began his escape. Adjusting his arms so that one held his weight, Justice wriggled his free arm into position so that he could move some of the dirt from the back of his head into the clear space beneath him. Packing down each handful, Justice thought of the king, of his life before he became the King's Man, of his horse standing ready in the evening sunlight. He thought of anything that came to mind in order to keep the terror of death at bay. Little by little, the mound beneath him rose. He worked patiently, carefully, knowing he could not afford to waste any space. The grave had not yet been deep enough for Wiley Oliver. If his calculations were right, he only needed to dig up through two feet of dirt before he was free. The dirt from his shoulders was added to the rising floor as Justice worked his way upward. Packing the dirt behind him as he moved ever so slowly upward. Time seemed to stand still as he painstakingly worked his way to freedom.

Justice's heart leaped as his hand felt the cool fall breeze. He was wedged in the dirt like an earthworm, but here was hope. Wriggling and digging his head soon burst through the surface. He gasped in the fresh air, scrambling frantically to free himself.

"They said you could not do it."

Justice planted his hands on the earth and pulled his

hips and legs through the hole. He stumbled in his haste to distance himself from what would have been his grave. Coughing and gasping for air, he kept moving away, unable to see through the dirt that covered his eyes. His hands were caked in dirt, and were no help in clearing his vision. Justice tripped and fell to the grass. Rolling onto his back he lay there drawing in large breaths of the clean air.

"They said you were dead, but I did not believe them."

Justice could not place the man's voice, but he knew whoever it belonged to was coming closer. He lay sprawled on the ground and let the stranger come.

"This will help," the man's words were followed by a wave of cold water in Justice's face.

Sitting up, Justice sputtered and gasped and tried to scoot away. The dirt, now turned to mud made it impossible to see. He wiped his hands fruitlessly on the wet grass where he had been laying and attempted to clear his eyes.

"Hmm, maybe not," the voice said. The footsteps retreated only to return once more.

Justice braced himself, but the second wave did not come. Instead, he felt something bump against his leg. Feeling cautiously, Justice discovered it was a bucket of water that had been set beside him. Getting to his knees, Justice plunged his hands in, freeing them from the grime of the earth. Next he cleaned his face rubbing and splashing until he could blink past the wetness and see! Relief washed over him, and he sat back to look up at the sky. The clouds were vibrant with color as the sun cast its last rays on them. Tears of gratitude sprung up and trailed their way down the assassin's cheeks. He was free.

"I did not believe them. That's why I stayed to see." The stranger repeated, unable to squelch his amazement at seeing Justice again.

With a heavy sigh, Justice wiped the tears from his face,

leaving muddy streaks in their wake. For the first time, he turned to the stranger. "Thank you for the water, sir." It was the younger man who had been present at Justice's burial.

"I'm Kore." He smiled at Justice who eyed him warily.

"Why did you help me now? You helped them bury me," Justice asked, searching the man's face.

"I did not help them," Kore countered.

"But you did not help me either and you were there," Justice pointed out. "Why?"

"For one thing, I'm not drunk. They were. Going against them would have meant both of us ending up in the hole," Kore pointed out casually. He picked up the shovel and went back to the hole.

Justice was surprised by the wave of panic he felt. "What are you doing?"

Kore heard the fear and glanced back at the professional killer who sat exhausted in the grass. He was a man like the rest of them. A man trying to make a living. Trying to serve the king.

"Don't panic, my good man," Kore began to dig. "I'm going to get that toothpick you carry in case someone else tries to lay you to rest before your time. I see they were not off by much when they thrust it in." Kore rambled on as he dug, "Milo thought he ran you through, but it looks like he almost missed you completely. You ought to wash the dirt out of that gash. It is not deep, but it is the little cuts people forget to take care of. I had a friend who lost an arm because of a scratch from a metal nail. Got him right about there." He paused to show Justice where the nail had scratched and stopped. Justice was no longer the weary man who had barely escaped death. Despite the dirt that covered him, he had risen to his feet and was once more the King's Man. The unavoidable assassin. He stood watching Kore dig with the uncanny calm that was his trademark. "You sure came out of that quick," Kore observed hesitantly. "Do you want me to keep digging for your sword or let it be?"

"You are almost to it. Try a little to the left," Justice answered. Calm, polite, and deadly. It was why he was feared.

"Sure, I will grab that for you." Kore was nervous now and talking to hide it. "See, I didn't dig you up because I thought the sword would have killed you. Milo put it in quick before I could say anything to stop him. They figured you were dead, or would be soon, so they left. I stayed. You are the only man alive I would have stayed to see. No one else could have done it." Kore stooped and felt around a little in the last divot he had made. As if by magic, he pulled Justice's gleaming sword from the earth. "There you go, as good as new. Just needs a little washing. You could use it too, you know."

"Thank you, Kore." Justice met his eyes, weighing the odds that the young man would cross him with his own sword.

As if he had read the assassin's thoughts, Kore turned the sword, holding it out by the hilt with the tip pointed at the ground. Justice stepped forward, his eyes only leaving Kore's for an instant as he took the sword.

"No hard feelings, right?" Kore asked stepping back. "I didn't help them bury you."

"I do not kill for my own benefit. Unless you commit a crime worthy of death and the king gives the command, you have no cause to fear my blade."

"Have you ever killed someone the king did not command you to kill?" Kore asked retrieving the bucket of muddy water.

"Never."

"That's a blessing at least. Some people are afraid you would."

"They are only afraid because they are guilty and deserve the punishment they dread." Justice pointed out, walking beside Kore toward the house.

"You still here?" The girl's voice met them before they

saw her in the dim doorway. "I saw the grave closed up and thought you had gone. I guess you forgot what the grave was for though." She pointed to the humped blanket that still covered Wiley Oliver's body. "Wasn't the hole for him?"

"Something came up," Kore answered before Justice could. "I'm Kore." He offered good-naturedly.

She studied him for a moment before performing an off balance curtsy, "Anna Lea. What do you mean something came up? It looks more like something fell in." She quipped looking at Justice. Dirt was falling off as he walked, but just as much was staying on him. His face, smeared with mud and blood, did not match the slightly pleasant expression he wore.

Justice paused and looked at Kore seriously, "Would you dig that hole again for Wiley's body?"

Kore glanced back at the filled in hole and then at Justice, covered in dirt. It was strange to suddenly see through a man he had been taught to fear. "I guess I don't mind," he said casually. "It will be easier the second time, now that you have loosened the dirt."

The relief in the assassin's eyes was thanks enough for Kore. Whistling, Kore headed back towards the grave, leaving Justice standing in the bare yard. A chicken scuttled past, breaking the silence. Anna Lea looked him over once more before going back inside, leaving Justice standing alone. He walked to the side of the house and whistled for his horse. The only sound was Kore's shovel breaking and throwing the dirt.

Milo would have his horse then. Justice sighed. It had been a long day. The sun was setting quickly, and he would travel much slower without his mount.

Making his way back across the yard, he stopped a few feet from the hole. "Do you know where Milo lives?"

Kore's head jerked upwards, and he locked eyes with

Justice. There was terror in his blue-green eyes.

Justice frowned slightly and stepped back. "I am not going to hurt you, Kore. I told you before that I do not kill for personal revenge."

Kore licked his lips nervously. "I…uh."

"I need my horse. If I'm not mistaken, Milo would be the one who took it."

"Yeah, probably Milo." Kore stuttered.

Justice put out his hand and Kore grasped it hesitantly. The hole was only a foot or so deep, but Justice helped Kore out onto equal ground.

"I don't understand you." Kore looked back at the shallow hole he had dug. "Why would you not get even? That must have been terrifying to be down there that long. The thought of it happening to me almost paralyzed me."

Shrugging and sending a shower of dirt from his clothes, Justice released his hand. "I serve the king. I do his bidding, not my own."

Kore frowned thoughtfully.

"However, there is the small matter of my horse. It is technically the king's horse, so if I could get it back…"

"I know where Milo lives."

Both men jumped and spun to face Anna Lea. She stood with a bundle over her shoulder and the chicken under her arm.

"I don't want to know." Justice stepped back. "I'm not taking you. I would ask at the tavern before I would ask you."

"That is ridiculous," Anna Lea countered, "They are trying to kill you. I can see you had some trouble with Milo and his men. What makes you think they will not try to finish the job?"

The men exchanged a glance.

"I will take you to Milo's." Anna Lea pressed.

"On what?" Justice asked.

Kore scratched his head, "Why are you taking the chicken?"

"This," Anna Lea lifted the bird slightly, causing it to cluck in protest, "is dinner."

"You thought of everything," Justice agreed in mock amazement. "But I'm still not going with you. You can take your chicken and your bundle and go right to the King's Highway. Take a left and walk until you see a sign for Weaver's Refuge. That's where you will want to be. It's a good place."

Kore nodded, "That is a great place. My mother went there after he…" He gestured at Justice and caught himself. "After her circumstances changed dramatically." He finished lamely without meeting their questioning looks.

"He killed your father?" Anna Lea asked in shock. "And you are digging graves for him?"

"It's complicated," Kore agreed. "I'll finish up and get out of your hair." Excusing himself, Kore returned to the grave where he dug vigorously.

Justice watched him thoughtfully, trying to remember who his father had been. Obviously Kore remembered the event. He was at least five years younger than Justice. Had he been there when the king's verdict was carried out?

"What did his father do?" Anna Lea asked softly.

"I don't know," Justice answered honestly. He turned to her and gave her a short, stiff bow, "Goodbye, Anna Lea." He strode quickly down the rutted trail he had arrived on towards the main road.

"Wait, aren't you going to help him bury Wiley?" Anna Lea called after him.

"No, bury your own dead."

CHAPTER 4

"Who are you here for?" the grizzly man pushed his way through the crowd that had gathered around Justice.

"I am not here for anyone," Justice replied. "I completed my assignment and am returning to the king."

"Been buried alive by the looks of him," another observed, adjusting his hat. "How did you escape?"

"He's not human, Finley. He probably sleeps in graves at night." The grizzly man shot back, eyeing Justice in the torchlight. "It is not safe to travel alone at night, but then I suppose you know that, being a hunter yourself."

"Yes, I am aware of that fact." It was poor timing to run into a merchant band returning from market. They had sold their goods and were returning home slightly intoxicated. Justice knew he should have turned off the road long before now. The band included three carts and six merchants to man them. Justice had been considering finding a place to wait out the night, when the men emerged from their inky camp by the road and surrounded him. Now, their torches lit the road and Justice stood stoically among them.

"You will stay with us tonight," Finley announced, much to the shock of the others in his party.

"Thank you, but no, I must continue on. I have been delayed already and will be expected back at the palace," Justice told them. He took a few steps, but no one moved aside. Stopping, he sized them up in the flickering light.

"You will stay with us tonight." Finley's tone was hard. A short blade glistened in the torchlight.

Justice weighed his options. It was his habit to avoid personal battles, if possible, but he had no desire to stay the night with the motley group around him.

"Traveling alone in these parts is dangerous." Grizzly was uncomfortably close to Justice. His breath reeked of onions, causing Justice to turn his face away.

Justice's hand moved toward the hilt of his sword. He saw no other option.

"Ah, there you are!" called a cheerful voice beyond the group. "Did you find a place to camp?"

Justice recognized Kore's voice at once. Why was the young man following him?

Kore barged his way into the little group. Clapping Grizzly on the shoulder, he leaned in confidentially. Whatever he said made the old man laugh. Kore laughed with him, apparently immune to the onion blast he had received.

"Just the two of you then?" Grizzly asked. "Won't you join our party? There's safety in numbers."

"Ah, but I wish we could. See, there's a young lady with us." Kore jerked a thumb over his shoulder. "We have to find better accommodations when there's a lady in tow." He sighed dreamily. "What I wouldn't give for a night with good company like yours under the stars."

"Let's see her." Finley held his torch higher revealing Anna Lea who stood shyly outside the ring of light they had created.

A few of the farmers whistled. "She's a good looking companion. Yours?" They shoved Kore good-naturedly. Kore laughed and looked embarrassed but did not deny it.

"We must be on our way, now. The lady is weary from her travels."

"You really shouldn't let her carry the bundle." Justice

squeezed from the circle and took the bundle from Anna Lea. "She's a brave lady to offer, but it is better for us to share the load." Anna Lea resisted him slightly, but Justice deftly removed the bundle from her slender hand and shouldered it himself.

"Leave the chicken to her though," Grizzly laughed. "She will know better what to make of it."

The group was a jolly one now and ready to laugh at the slightest hint of humor. Clapping each other and the strangers on the back, they sent the King's Man and his companions off into the darkness with a rousing song ringing out behind them.

Justice walked in silence ahead of the other two. All his life, he had traveled alone. He was feared or hated wherever he went. The only one he ever loved had been murdered in revenge by a man Justice had later killed for the king. That grudge was even, but the pain of it never left him. Justice was an assassin, not because he enjoyed it, but because he could picture his wife's murderer in the face of every man he killed. For each murderer had deprived someone else of a person they loved. Each one had hurt another as Justice had once been hurt himself.

"I can take the bundle back," Anna Lea offered quietly. "Looks like you have something heavy on your mind."

Justice shook his head. Being buried alive had rattled him. His mind, in order to escape the terror as he struggled for life, had gone back over events Justice thought he had forgotten. "I will carry it a while longer. After all, you two saved me from an unpleasant encounter. I do not have your good-natured appeal, Kore. What did you say to the man?"

Kore grinned, enjoying the praise. "Nothing important. A bit of a jest to get them laughing." Kore made a disgusted face and rubbed his nose. "His breath nearly knocked me out. Never have I smelled onions so strongly!"

Justice couldn't help chuckling at Kore's reenactment.

"I thought maybe you could not smell," Justice admitted, still smiling.

"You look good when you smile," Anna Lea observed.

Justice's smile disappeared.

"And leave it to a girl to spoil the moment," Kore groaned.

"What?" Anna Lea looked from one to the other.

"Imagine you are enjoying a group of friends, laughing and talking and whatever girls do." Kore paused, "Got the picture?"

"Yes?" She glanced at Justice who was staring with that irritatingly calm and slightly pleasant look into the darkness.

"Now, dear lady, imagine a man walks into your group and informs you that you have some type of food scrap lodged between two of your teeth." Kore made an unpleasant face and dramatically pointed at his teeth. "Feel that? That is what you have just done to our good friend yonder. Enjoy the moment. Don't scrutinize your companions."

She looked irritated but said nothing more.

"How far is the next town?" Kore asked, closing the distance between Justice and himself.

"Not far."

"You said that ages ago," Anna Lea complained. "Do you even know where the town is?"

"Yes, but I am not going to the town. I am getting my horse."

Kore and Anna Lea both stopped walking.

"You are what?" Kore demanded. "I saved you from those men so you could get yourself killed by Milo?"

"Apparently so," Justice answered without feeling. "I told you when I left I was getting my horse. It belongs to the king."

"Screw the horse and the king!" Kore would have said more but Justice's strong hand around his neck stopped him. "I didn't mean it, Justice. Honest. I wasn't thinking. I didn't mean it."

"Don't you ever disrespect the king in my presence," Justice breathed, his eyes glinting in the pale light of the thin moon. "No, I won't," Kore promised. "I didn't mean it, Justice. Honest. I guess I am tired and was not thinking straight. I like the king. Honest I do."

Justice released Kore as suddenly as he grabbed him. Stalking off down the barely visible road, he disappeared into the blackness.

Kore sat down by the road and rubbed his throat. "He's a strange one."

"Why are we trying to travel with him?" Anna Lea asked. Suddenly she leaped up. "My bundle! He..." Her words trailed off as she spotted the bundle by the side of the road. Justice had dropped it there when he grabbed Kore. "Never mind." She reached for it wearily.

Kore, who had jumped up at her exclamation, took it from her and slung in onto his back. "I will carry it for a while. You have the chicken."

———

Justice moved through the darkness without a sound. He walked upright, confident, as he approached the quiet house. His hand touched the rough wood of Milo's homemade fence. Justice stopped to listen. Nothing, not even a dog to guard the stock. His whistle, soft as it was, carried well in the stillness. A slight smile appeared on Justice's face when he heard the soft, answering neigh of his mount. Slipping over the fence, he made his way across the field. A sound from the house stopped him.

Drawing back into the shadows, Justice watched as the silhouette of the big man slipped from the house and disappeared into the barn. It was evident that Milo had his own doubts about the finality of Justice's death. Or perhaps, he believed the king had sent another man to retrieve the horse and right the wrong that had been done.

Justice gave another soft, low whistle, which was answered by a muffled snort. Now, Milo was inside, waiting for him, keeping the horse quiet to draw Justice inside.

Justice moved to the side of the barn. The edge of the roof extended outward on either side of the barn to offer shade and shelter for the animals in the field outside the barn. Justice stepped into the shadows and waited. There was a muffled shuffling from inside the barn. His mount knew he was close and wanted to come to him, but something held him back. Passing two of the side windows, Justice peered into the third without putting his head through the opening. There was no light in the barn. The rustling came from the first stall, the one closest to the barn door. Taking hold of the rafter just above the opening, Justice lifted his legs and slipped feet first through the window into the barn. The horses movements grew more agitated, and a muffled whinny broke the stillness.

Justice waited, giving Milo time to get impatient. The barn was pitch black inside. The feeble moonlight could not find its way through the sheltered windows. His horse was moving freely now, stomping around the stall and scraping impatiently at the door with a hoof. Still, Justice crouched in the empty stall, waiting. Footsteps came toward him, heavy, for they belonged to a big man.

After several minutes had passed, Milo broke the stillness. "It's you, isn't it?" He paused, waiting for the answer that never came. "Kore dug you up, huh? I should have known better. I knew he would circle back. He doesn't have the guts for killing. Not since you took care of his old man."

"No one dug me up," Justice answered. His voice sounded

eerie in the darkness.

"How do I know it is really you?"

Justice could tell by the slight tremble in the big man's voice that he had no doubt about who had spoken. He made no answer.

"What now?" Milo's tone was hard, but the tremor remained. "You know that only one of us can walk away alive tonight. Are you willing to face me like a man, or are you going to hide in the shadows like a coward."

Justice knew many men who would have burst out angrily at the insult. However, Justice was not there for his own honor, and once more gave no answer. He moved across the barn, carefully letting Milo's voice drown out any sound he made.

"Come and face me, Assassin!" Milo was losing his nerve. In the daylight, drunk and backed by his friends, he would stand up to anyone. But here in the darkness, confronted by the assassin, he thought he had killed, Milo's courage gave out. "Alright, Justice. You can have the horse. I'll give it to you without a fight. You won this round and can go back to your pretty little palace on the mountain."

"You seem to forget that you buried me alive," Justice pointed out.

Startled, the big man spun around to face the voice. How had the assassin crossed the barn? "You did not get out of the grave." Milo's eyes widened in the darkness. "You are a ghost!"

"Perhaps I am," Justice had once more changed his position. "I am here for the king's horse."

Milo hurried to the first stall and took the rag from over the horse's muzzle. The horse, a large dark animal, shook his head and moved away, seeming to Milo to merge with the blackness of the barn and disappear.

"Take him!" The panic was more evident now as the big man backed towards the door of his barn.

"Saddle him," Justice ordered. "All that belongs to the

king must be returned."

Milo hurried to obey. The horse, unfamiliar with the big man's ways, shied and moved about nervously as the tack was put in place. Once the task was done, Milo opened the barn door and backed out through the thin beam of moonlight that illuminated him. The horse, feeling himself freed at last, galloped through the open door.

A whistle brought the big animal to an abrupt halt. It turned and trotted back to the door of the barn. Milo, from the safety of his porch, watched in horror as a shadowy figure emerged from the barn and mounted the animal. "It cannot be. I thrust the sword into him myself," Milo muttered under his breath. "It cannot be."

Without a word, the ghostly rider thundered off into the night.

CHAPTER 5

"It was rotten of him to leave us like this," Anna Lea complained. She was finding it harder and harder to lift her feet, which caused her to stumble often.

"He is used to caring for only himself. The king's missions are all that matter to him." Kore, too, had been hurt by the sudden disappearance of the King's Man. Kore knew that if he had not stepped in, there would have been a knife fight between the Merchants and Justice. Though they outnumbered him, Justice had his sword again and would not be inclined to bow to their wishes.

"Can't we stop, only for a few minutes?" asked Anna Lea with a groan.

"It is very dangerous along this road. Many are killed and robbed, for there is no way to track the murderer. We cannot afford to be killed in our sleep." Kore pointed out, trying to add humor to the situation.

"I don't care if robbers do find us," Anna Lea said stubbornly as she sat on the side of the road. "I cannot, and will not, go a step farther."

"Do be reasonable, Anna Lea," Kore pleaded. "A few more hours and the sun will start lighting the sky. I know there is a town ahead. If we did not miss the turn."

"Are you trying to be comforting?" Anna Lea asked, removing one of her shoes and rubbing her foot. "I can't go a step farther. You can go on to that fictional town ahead if you like."

"He wouldn't dare to leave a poor, defenseless lady like you out here on the road," a cruel voice said from the blackness behind Anna Lea. She shoved her foot back into her shoe and scrambled up to stand by Kore.

"Who are you?" she asked with a strange, nervous giggle.

"No need to fear." The man who emerged from the rocks along the road was hard to make out. He was short and wide. It appeared to Anna Lea that his teeth were missing on one side of his mouth.

"What do you want?" Kore asked, putting Anna Lea behind himself. "We are not wealthy travelers," Kore told him quickly.

"No?"

"Our greatest treasure at the moment is the lady's chicken." Kore took the sleeping bird from Anna Lea. "You are welcome to it."

"We will see about that." The first robber answered. He cocked his head toward Kore and three more men materialized from the dark shadows cast by the towering rocks. They moved around Kore, their cruel faces eager. One man fingered Anna Lea's soft hair.

"They think I'm pretty." The snorting laugh that came from Anna Lea made everyone, even Kore, step back in surprise.

"She's a simpleton, isn't she," The leader observed her with disgust. "You were probably hoping some robber along the way would take her off your hands." He laughed and the others grinned maliciously. "You will have no luck there," the leader went on. "We are only interested in your money. Even the simplest of travelers carry a few coins for their journey." He nodded at his men who moved around Kore once more.

"Let them go." Justice's voice was commanding.

Everyone turned to stare at the dark rider that moved steadily nearer. I am a King's Man. You have no right to these travelers. Robbing travelers on the King's Highway brings a severe punishment," Justice reminded them firmly.

"Only if you can catch us," The leader spat angrily. At his signal, the four disappeared once more among the scattered rocks.

Justice's mount stopped beside the open-mouthed companions. He dismounted and turned to Anna Lea. "Anna Lea, you will ride to the town. You have traveled well tonight."

She glanced at Kore who nodded dumbly. The horse was a tall, well-built animal. As soon as she touched the stirrup, she knew it was too high and wondered how Justice, who was only marginally taller than her, managed to mount. She glanced at him and found he was watching her with that same amused expression.

"How do I?" Anna Lea fell silent as Justice dropped to one knee beside the horse and offered her his hand. Taking his hand, she stepped gingerly onto his knee and mounted quickly.

"You are not as simple as you pretended to be among the robbers," Justice observed handing up the chicken. "I recall you also played the simpleton very well when you were held captive by Wiley Oliver."

Anna Lea took the bird but did not meet his eyes. Wiley Oliver had been a cruel man and treated her as a slave. Pretending she did not understand had seemed to amuse him and lessen the blows.

Kore looked up from his task of strapping her bundle to the back of the saddle. It was true that Anna Lea seemed to be a different person than the one he had seen sometimes at the market with Wiley. He wondered why he had not noticed it before. Taking the reins, Justice moved the horse forward. Kore fell in step on the other side of the horse's head. Both walked in silence, lost in their own thoughts.

On top of the horse, Anna Lea lifted her eyes and saw

the stars twinkling above her. Until that moment, the realization that she was free had not set in. Now, as the strong muscles of the horse moved beneath her, she felt a swell of emotions. She was free!

———

Anna Lea startled awake and sat up in the saddle. She was sore and stiff and wondered how long she had slept against the gentle horse's neck. She rubbed her eyes and looked down at her companions. The first rays of the sun were drenching the world with their soft light, but the men did not notice the beauty.

Justice and Kore walked steadily, without speaking. They had traveled all night and were exhausted. The road sign promised there would be an inn only one mile ahead, but even this was not enough to quicken their weary steps.

"There it is!" Anna Lea called excitedly from her vantage point. "Up there on the right, in that stand of trees. How wonderful a hot bath will feel!" She looked down at Justice and fell silent. The man was still covered in dirt, the wound on his face was dark with dried blood mixed with dirt. In the last twenty-four hours, he had killed a man, been buried alive, faced hostile travelers, stolen back the king's horse, faced bandits, and walked through the night so that she could ride. On the other side was Kore, silently suffering with an ill-fitting pair of shoes. He had said nothing but she had noticed early on that he tried to twist the leather about to ease the pain when he thought she was not looking. Though they had nothing in common, one day was all it had taken to bring them together in an unlikely band.

They turned off the road and made their way to the inn, keeping the same steady, mind-numbing pace. As soon as her feet touched the ground, the innkeeper's wife rushed forward to greet her and bring her inside. The gentle woman promised a hot bath and a good meal. Anna Lea glanced behind her to see Justice leading his mount stoically towards the stables. He was a man under orders, and the interests of the king always came first.

CHAPTER 6

"There you are!" Anna Lea said cheerily as she crossed the crowded dining room that filled the first floor of the inn. She wore a borrowed dress that did not fit her well, but did not seem to mind the spacious gown. She was clean and rested which put her in a very good mood. Justice and Kore had also bathed, and both looked refreshed. The long wound on Justice's cheek was swollen and red, but he gave no indication of pain. They had slept through the morning and were joining together again for the midday meal. "I was not sure where I would find you."

Kore looked up from his food with a scowl. "As if you had to look. These wretched people have not given us a moment's peace since we came in." He raised his voice and added, "All we want to do is eat in peace," for the benefit of the hecklers.

Across from him, Justice sat calmly eating his food. "You could sit at another table," he suggested, his voice low.

Kore's scowl deepened, "I am traveling with you, and I am sitting with you." He shoved a bite of potato into his mouth, shooting deadly glares at the other customers.

"Do you mind if I sit with you?" Anna Lea asked, when neither of her companions offered her a chair.

Instinctively, both men rose at her question.

"If you don't mind the side show," Kore responded with irritation.

Taking his seat once more, Justice watched as Kore pulled

out the chair beside him and she sat.

Justice smiled to himself. Both Kore and Anna Lea had obviously had some form of courtly training. He wondered again who Kore's father had been. The young man's face was not familiar. Justice shrugged it off as he cut himself another bite. He rarely knew the men he killed. It was better that way.

The other travelers shouted everything from threats to insults. One recounted again and again how he had watched Justice kill his only son. They called him low and degrading things, but never once did Justice even spare them a glance.

"How do you stand it?" Kore asked over the noise.

Justice's shrug was barely noticeable.

Anna Lea covered her ears, trying to block out the terrible account of the lifeless eyes of the man's son.

Justice stood, and the room went silent instantly. He looked from face to face, and they cowered in silence before him. Without a word, he turned and walked from the dining hall and up the stairs.

There was a stunned silence for several minutes after he left. Kore and Anna Lea exchanged a confused look. How was it that the people could throw insults so freely at one they so obviously feared?

The noise in the room resumed at a low murmur, gradually rising to a normal level once more. It was as if they had forgotten the assassin completely.

Kore waved over the owner and asked for a plate for Anna Lea. She sat stunned, staring at the worn wooden tabletop before her.

"You okay?" Kore asked, when her food had been delivered and she made no effort to eat it.

"Is it always like that for him?" she asked softly.

Kore studied the grain of the table thoughtfully. "I don't know. If it is, I do not know how he bears it. I am not a swordsman, but if I had the skill he has, I fear I would destroy the whole roomful for such a rude display. You should eat. I hope we can leave this place at once."

A muscular, well-bearded man dressed in black came up behind them and touched Anna Lea's damp hair. "What is a beauty like you doing in a place like this?" he asked condescendingly.

"Isn't it quaint?" Anna Lea asked turning to face him. "Such a sweet place all full of people eating together. My Pa sometimes lets me come here to eat. But only if I wear my best dress. Do you like it?" She paused, looking at him as if she actually expected him to compliment the baggy borrowed dress.

"It might as well be a sack you are wearing," the dark man answered scornfully. "Travel with me, and I will show you beautiful things."

Anna Lea laughed. It was a shocking, annoying snorting affair that caused Kore to stare. The bearded man stepped back in disgust.

"Travel with you? What would my Pa say?" Again, the loud, snorting giggle escaped from her lips. She covered her mouth, but the muffled sound continued.

"Silence!" the stranger boomed.

Anna Lea cowered, and fell silent, her eyes wide with fright.

He turned on Kore. "I have seen you before. Where are you heading?"

Kore glanced at the man's hand, resting on the hilt of the sword he wore. The sword bore the emblem of the king. On his finger was the matching ring of a King's Man. Kore's gaze traveled from the hilt to the hard eyes of the stranger. "I am finding my way in the world. I have no destination as of yet."

"You are traveling with him?" His disdain for Justice was clear as he gestured toward the stairs.

"Yes." Kore tried to hide the fear he felt.

"You have not traveled with him long. I see you are wondering why he sits in silence and why they jeer at him, a King's Man." His voice carried well, and others stopped talking to listen.

Kore glanced around. "Yes, I would like to know." He said honestly. Beside him, Anna Lea was stirring her food together on her plate. Now and then she would take a hesitant bite. Each time she would make a face and stir it more.

The King's Man glanced at her odd behavior and sneered. "It is because they do not fear him." He boomed. "Justice is a weak man who does only the king's bidding."

"You have the ring and sword of a King's Man. Do you not do the king's bidding?" Kore asked.

He laughed scornfully. "Of course, I do, but I allow no man to cross me. No one here would dare to mock me." He scanned the room, and everyone did their best not to meet his eye. "You see, Justice does not fight for himself. He kills his man and runs back to his king with his tail between his legs. It is rumored that his sword has never been drawn in his own defense."

"And so they scorn him but fear the day their name is on the letter he bears?" Kore asked, hating the cowards for their cruelty.

"Brutus! I thought you would come." Justice gave the man a rare but insincere smile as he crossed the room to their table. "Are you two still eating?" He glanced questioningly at Anna Lea's odd stirring and nibbling, but said nothing about it.

"I think she is almost done," Kore looked at the soupy mess she had created out of a perfectly good plate of chicken, potatoes, and beans. "Are we leaving?" He rose eagerly.

"Not yet. I heard Brutus and thought I would come down. He is always good for a yarn or two. I do think he missed his calling as a minstrel. He seems to love to entertain the simpleminded." Justice met Brutus' eyes. There was a shared animosity between them that was almost tangible.

"I thought you had retreated for the evening," Brutus answered with narrowed eyes.

"No, sadly for you, I am here for a while longer." Justice took his seat once more across from Kore. Though he leaned one arm easily on the table, Brutus knew Justice well enough to know he could strike at a moment's notice. But would he? Brutus did not dare to test him. Never had a man, no matter how wicked, been able to overcome Justice when he came for them.

"Nasty cut. Was your last killing more than you could handle?" Brutus scoffed.

Justice did not respond. He sat back, cocking one elbow over the back of the chair beside him. A group of men at a nearby table started a hushed but still audible, story about the cruel, cowardly King's Man. It was obvious by their glances and sneers that they were referring to Justice. Not a man dared to speak ill of Brutus. They knew it could cost them their life.

"For a King's Man you are taking a chance traveling here on the outskirts of the kingdom," Brutus observed. "A half day's ride will take any fugitive to safety across the border, say someone fleeing after killing a coward."

"Has someone threatened you, Brutus?" Justice asked casually.

Brutus fumed, and his hand moved to the hilt of his sword once more.

The door opened, and Justice glanced up. He locked eyes with the thin rat-like man who had held his sword at his burial. Rats' beady eyes bulged with surprise, and he retreated the way he had come.

Justice glanced at Kore, but the young man's back was to the door, and he had not seen the thin man.

"Always about the king's business aren't you, Justice?"

Brutus was sore and wanted a reason to fight. "Tell me why you are here on the outskirts of the kingdom. Has your precious king cast you away? Why don't you flee back to the safety of his shadow?"

Justice said nothing. He was waiting for something, but no one knew what.

The jeers went on. A bold peasant made a broad insult which included all who wore the king's ring. Brutus' sword was at his throat in an instant. "Do you dare to mock me?" he demanded. The man, his eyes wide, was quick to apologize. When the blade was lowered, he hurried from the room.

The noon meal was over, and the men started to leave in groups of two and three. Dishes were stacked up and carried to the kitchen where the scraps would be scraped into a pail for the hogs out back. A few men sat talking together in little bunches. Kore could tell they were expecting a fight between the King's Men and did not want to miss it.

Through it all, Anna Lea kept on her mindless stirring and eating. Now and then, she would glance up at Brutus and give him a queer smile which unnerved him. Kore was beginning to wonder if she really had lost her mind.

The door opened and a man entered. His hair was gray, but he bore no other sign of old age. His brown eyes quickly took in the room.

"Ah, Doctor, you have arrived at last." Justice stood and went to greet the doctor.

Kore turned in his seat to survey the newcomer. It struck him that the man appeared to be anything but pleased at the sight of Justice. The doctor glanced past Justice and met the eyes of Brutus.

"You have a nasty cut, it appears to have the signs of infection," the doctor observed distractedly, still glancing at Brutus now and then.

"I was hoping you could take a look at it," Justice confided. "I heard you were in the area and might come here for an early dinner."

The doctor looked at Justice with a stiff expression. "You did not pay me for the last treatment, Justice."

Justice blinked at the doctor in surprise. "You told me not to pay you. You said the king pays you and refused the money I offered."

Brutus gave a mocking laugh, "The king does not pay him. You know that as well as I do."

"You told me he did." The pleasantness had left Justice's face. Ignoring Brutus, he went on. "I offered you payment, and you declined it."

"And why did you not go to the king and complain?" Brutus asked the doctor with a taunting smile.

The doctor looked embarrassed. "I could not go to him without casting a shadow on his favorite man. I knew he would not listen to me if I brought a complaint about his beloved Justice."

Justice was caught in the crossfire. The men who had waited for a show now watched the pair eagerly, openly enjoying the discomfort of their enemy.

"If you have chosen to go back on your word, I will give you the payment." Justice was frowning darkly at the man he thought to have been a friend. "I do not have the full amount with me as I am returning from my assignment." Justice put his hand to his pouch and pulled out the coins it held. "I have thirty with me. I can give you twenty-five now. The rest I owe to the innkeeper for our stay. He too is not paid by the king."

"No, keep your money," the doctor protested with an offended air. "I won't be called a liar before my friends."

"You live here then?" Justice asked incredulously. "Here, on the outskirts? And with him." Justice jerked his thumb in Brutus' direction.

The doctor glanced once more past Justice at Brutus but did not answer.

Justice's frown deepened, and his eyes narrowed. "You are a traitor to your king. You have come here to use the power of his name to accomplish your own wishes."

"How dare you insult a servant of the king!" Brutus surged forward, his sword drawn. It clashed sharply with Justice's blade, and the two men stood facing each other. Each daring the other to strike again.

"Come now, put your swords away," the doctor pleaded. "Justice, I will look at your wound. There is no need to pay me. It will be payment enough to treat the king's special pet."

"Very well, I will give you that pleasure." Justice stepped back from Brutus, and both men sheathed their swords, eyeing one another warily. "I will pay you the twenty-five now and send the rest by messenger upon my return to the palace." Justice strode across the room. The doctor, with a pleased glance at Brutus, hurried after him. Brutus ran a hand over his beard. His eyes had not lost their murderous gleam as he watched Justice climb the stairs once more.

Now that the action was over, the rest of the men hurried out to tell what they had seen. Brutus turned in time to catch sight of one of Anna Lea's queer smiles. He glared at her and stalked from the room.

They waited, watching the bustling servants who could never seem to work fast enough to please the Innkeeper. He shouted and fumed at them, while they hurried to clear the tables. The sunlight moved slowly on the floor and yet they sat. The light had just touched the leg of the table when the doctor, looking pleased, descended the stairs. He spoke briefly to the Innkeeper and hurried out. Kore glanced at Anna Lea who was still stirring but no longer eating and excused himself, muttering something about Justice.

Anna Lea glanced around and found only the innkeeper

and a few servants remained. She set down her fork and rose to return to her room.

CHAPTER 7

Kore knocked lightly on the door of the room he shared with Justice. A questioning grunt came from inside. Pushing open the door, Kore saw Justice, lying on his back on the far bed. His face was turned away from the door, but he did not bother to look and see who had entered. A bandage covered the long wound on his face.

"What did the doctor say?" Kore asked softly, wondering at the fortitude of the lone man. Here was a King's Man who truly loved his king and who suffered greatly for it. Yet, Brutus, who used the king's name only for his own gain, was respected by all because of his cruelty.

"It will heal." Justice's voice sounded tight and strange.

Kore sat on the bed by the door. "Why do you do it, Justice? Why do you serve the king when it costs you so much."

"He is worthy of my service," Justice responded with feeling. "He is good and true and upholds the laws that protect our land."

"But they do not care, and because of them you are lying there penniless and bleeding." Kore lay back and put his hands behind his head. Glancing across the room at where Justice lay, he was sorry for what he had said. Justice needed someone to stand beside him, not to criticize him. Not knowing what to say, Kore said nothing.

"We must leave here," Justice said after a long pause.

Kore propped himself on his elbow, "Now?"

"Very soon," was Justice's vague answer.

Kore frowned, "But why?"

Justice sighed wearily. "Rats came in not long before the doctor. Brutus is right. The border is close and many a man would eagerly kill me to gain favor with Brutus. He is like a king here, and those who fear the king have flocked to him for protection."

"Then why did you come here?" Kore asked sitting up. "If you knew all that, why did you bring us here?"

Justice was silent for so long that Kore thought he would not answer the question. He lay back again, knowing there was a long walk ahead.

"I needed the doctor." Justice's voice was strained once more. "I thought he was still loyal to the king."

"Surely Anna Lea could have treated you, or even I could have cleaned it. Why come here, where you knew you could be killed?"

"The king needed to know if the doctor was still loyal to him. Rumors had reached him and our king never acts without confirming the facts."

"So he sends you to get killed so he can be sure about the doctor?" Kore's tone was incredulous.

"I warned you before not to speak ill of the king," Justice reminded him firmly. "You do not know him as I do."

"Alright, I am not speaking against him." Kore rolled so his back was to Justice. "Wake me up when we are leaving."

"I will take you as far as the Weaver's Refuge, then you will be on your own."

"Great," Kore huffed in irritation. "If we get out at all."

———

Kore woke with a start. The room was dark. Scrambling to

his feet he saw someone standing in the shadows by the door.

"Who's there?" Kore demanded.

"A little jumpy are we?" Justice asked from behind him. "Try not to shout. The goal is to leave without making a fuss." Though he spoke softly, Kore could hear that Justice's voice was strong and sure again. The rest had been good for them all.

Kore kept his eyes on the shadowy figure. "But who...?"

The figure removed its's hood and he could make out the thick wavy hair that fell to her shoulders.

"Anna Lea? What are you doing in here?"

"She is traveling with us to the Weaver's Refuge." There was amusement in Justice's voice. "Or had you forgotten?"

"No one wakes me or tells me anything," Kore muttered. He looked around his bed, but as he had fallen asleep in his clothes there was nothing for him to gather.

On the floor beside Anna Lea was her bundle. The chicken was in the barn with Justice's horse.

Justice went to the window and peered out. Moonlight dimly illuminated his features. The bandage was gone, and his face was marred by the ugly swollen gash that ran across his cheek from his hairline to his chin.

Justice turned and caught Kore staring at him. He frowned questioningly, but Kore only looked away.

"Come, we must hurry." He went to the door and opened it softly. Once he was satisfied that the hall was clear, he beckoned them to follow. Kore took Anna Lea's bag and motioned for her to follow Justice. He could not forget her strange behavior at the midday meal.

She crept out after Justice, and Kore followed close behind. They let themselves out through the side door of the inn and waited in the shadows.

No one dared to move. A cloud passed over the moon and Justice moved quickly across the clearing. The others followed silently. Crouching in the dark shadow of a large tree, Justice waited until they were beside him.

"I will get the horse. If I do not succeed, you must take Anna Lea to the Weaver's Refuge."

Kore opened his mouth to protest, but Anna Lea shook her head and he closed it again.

Justice made his way to the barn, his movements easy and silent. In minutes, they lost sight of him completely though the sliver of the moon was visible once more.

There was a commotion, and Kore touched Anna Lea's arm. Together they ran across to the mouth of the road and hid behind the thick trunk of a tree. They watched breathlessly as the minutes ticked by. The night sounds resumed, and the clouds once more covered the moon.

Anna Lea leaned close to Kore's ear, "How do we…?"

Her question was interrupted by the startled squawk of a chicken.

"He's bringing the chicken." Her eyes sparkled with silent laughter.

"Is he mad?" Kore clinched his teeth. Had Justice given up? Was he trying to get killed?

Soft hoof beats answered his silent questions.

"The guard will wake soon. Be quick," Justice hissed, holding the horse's head. The stirrups had been lowered and Anna Lea mounted easily. Justice handed her the chicken, which was wrapped in a cloth to keep it silent, and moved the horse forward. It seemed the beast understood the need to be silent, for it placed its big hooves softly as it walked. Kore grabbed the bundle and hurried after them.

CHAPTER 8

Anna Lea stood up in the stirrups and looked around in the blackness. The rest had done her good. Unlike the night before, she was alert and eager to see what lay ahead. Hope fluttered inside her. Perhaps she was actually free. She had been held captive so long that she had almost lost all hope of tasting freedom again. Sitting in the saddle once more, she looked down at the men who flanked her mount. They were not like the captors she had known. The others had treated her like a slave and beat her if she did not meet their expectation. They were also not like Brutus who saw her only as something to possess and throw away. Justice and Kore had gone out of their way to help her. Even paying extra so that she could have a room of her own at the inn. It seemed as if they wanted to help her, not for what they would gain, but because of some inner kindness.

"Kore?"

He glanced up at her. "Hmm?"

"Who was your father?" Anna Lea asked.

"No one," Kore answered.

"The way you carry yourself says differently," Justice observed from the other side of the horse. "You are a man used to a finer life, to courtly behavior and kindness."

"You do not remember him then?" Kore asked.

"No, I seldom know those I am sent to kill."

"How do you know they are guilty?" Anna Lea was looking up at the stars as she spoke. "No disrespect to the king, but what if he made a mistake?"

"When I killed Wiley Oliver, what did I ask him?" Justice asked.

Anna Lea thought back, "You asked him if he had killed the counselor and his wife." Her voice wavered slightly as she spoke.

"And how did he respond?"

There was a moment's pause before they heard Anna Lea's thoughtful answer. "He said he had."

"I am not sent on a whim or a hunch." Justice confirmed. "The king is just."

"Is it hard be become a King's Man?" Kore glanced over to see Justice's reaction.

Justice considered the question before answering. "The training is vigorous, but when you love the king, obeying him brings great pleasure." Justice smiled at Kore's confused look. "It is hard to understand when you do not know him."

"Do you think I could become one?"

"A King's Man?" Justice was looking at Kore, without actually seeing him. He knew the young man had been impressed by the bold power of Brutus and the fearful respect given to Justice when he met someone's eyes. Being a King's Man was not made up of these shows of power. It came from a submissive love for the king. "I think so," Justice answered at length. "If you truly learned to love the king. But first you must become his subject. This is something Brutus never did, and why he serves himself as much or more than he serves the king. He is a King's Man in name alone."

Kore was taken back by the statement. "But aren't we all his subjects?"

"No, that is a common misunderstanding." Justice stroked the neck of the horse, enjoying the chance to relax and speak of the king. "We are all born into his realm, but that alone does not make you his subject."

"I was born here and that makes me a subject," Kore crossed his arms stubbornly.

He did not see Anna Lea grinning from above at his childish behavior. "How do you become a subject?" she asked.

"You ask the king to make you one. It is an honor that is free to all who ask." Justice's eyes shone with love for his king.

Kore humphed.

With a glance in Kore's direction, Justice explained, "The king's realm is his reach of power. There is no land beyond his power. Even the outskirts where people think they will escape his judgment, is a place of judgement itself. It is a terrible place without love or kindness and thus continually filled with pain and sorrow."

"But I know a man who chose to go to the outskirts. He was not being punished by the king," Kore pointed out.

"Separation itself is a terrible punishment. Have you seen him since he left?"

Kore's stubborn look melted into one of curiosity. "No, I have not."

Looking at the road ahead, Justice did not press the issue.

"But if we are all born under the king's power, how is it different to be his subject?" Anna Lea inquired.

"His subjects are those who have chosen to serve him as their king. Their names are written in the king's book, and he sends help to them when he knows they are in need."

"If the king is like you," Anna Lea's words came slowly and thoughtfully, "then I would like to become a subject of the king." She met his gaze shyly.

"The king's goodness and kindness surpass my own by..." Justice searched for the right word. "There is no measure to express it. There is no one who can even compare to his greatness."

Anna Lea smiled, "I feel that I love him a little already."

Justice stopped and put his hand up to her. Eyes shining with happiness, she clasped his hand firmly.

"Anna Lea, I publically recognize you as a loyal subject to the king."

Kore rolled his eyes and walked on.

———

The sun was well up when Justice drew their attention to a speck of a man far ahead. They examined him as he came closer.

"It is a king's messenger." Kore looked past the horse's head at Justice. "What does he want?"

"We will know soon enough," Justice answered as the man approached.

"Justice, I am so glad I found you. I have a message from the king." The messenger was dusty and weary from his journey. He pulled a letter from his pouch and handed it to the assassin.

Anna Lea felt a shiver run through her. It was identical to the one Justice had read to Wiley Oliver. The red wax stood out sharply against the white paper.

Justice took the letter and examined the seal. The sun had been up for several hours, and they welcomed a break by the road. Anna Lea dismounted, and Kore noticed for the first time that she had changed back into the working dress she had worn when he met her.

"Have I grown an extra head?" Anna Lea quipped, putting her hands on her hips.

"No," Kore looked away, embarrassed. "I did not realize you had changed."

She laughed, a pleasant melodious sound with no re-semblance to the snorting exhibition she had given at the inn. "Into this old thing?" she grinned at him. "The sun is getting to your brain, good sir."

Justice was inspecting the letter, turning it this way and that in the sunlight.

"It's been a long journey," the messenger hinted, attempting to dust himself off. "And it is a long way back."

"Then I suggest you get started." Justice looked at him suspiciously. "Who gave you this letter?"

The messenger stood straighter. "The king himself gave me that letter. It might be a little worn because my horse threw a shoe and sent me flying. It has taken me some time to locate you. It is a long journey from the palace. You are not far from the border you know."

"Yes, I know." Justice met the messenger's greedy eyes. "Perhaps, since you are returning to the king, you can spare a few coins. It seems our purses are light today."

The messenger looked shocked and then offended. Without another word he turned away sharply and marched off down the road.

Anna Lea laughed. "What a funny man. All the time hoping to glean a few coins off of you, Justice. You set him straight. Though I do wish he had money to spare. I'm famished."

Justice's smile was genuine. "Thanks to your foresight, My Lady, you have a meal under your arm, if you are willing to work for it."

Anna Lea looked surprised and pulled the cloth back from the drowsy chicken.

Justice turned away from them. His face grew serious again, and he tapped the letter against his hand thoughtfully.

"I'll make the fire," Kore offered eagerly. It had been a long night, and they were all hungry.

While they set to work, Justice sat on a rock in the shade, still tapping the letter against his hand.

"Why don't you open it?" Kore asked, as he passed with

a bundle of wood under his arm.

Justice looked up without moving his head. "I will."

"I guess something like that takes a little preparation." Kore observed, continuing on to the little fire pit he had created with a ring of stones.

Anna Lea was expertly plucking the dead chicken while Kore coaxed his fire to life. As occupied as they were, both were aware the instant the seal of the letter was broken. They stole furtive glances at Justice as he read, watching his face for any clue to what the letter said. To their disappointment, his face gave nothing away. He folded the letter and began the thoughtful tapping again.

"Good news?" Kore asked. He was going for more wood as an excuse to pass by where Justice sat.

"Not exactly. But it is on the way."

Kore was chilled by the calm words which meant death.

"Who is it?" Kore asked, forgetting the wood.

"I do not know him." The thoughtful frown remained, and Justice did not look up at Kore.

"Like you did not know my father?"

"Yes."

Kore moved closer, "Do you ever wonder if you killed the wrong man?" It was not an accusation, just a question.

"No."

"But like Anna Lea said last night, what if the man is innocent?"

The letter stopped tapping and Justice faced Kore. "Kore, was your father innocent?"

Kore looked away, "No."

"If your father had lived, would more innocent people have died because of him?"

Kore nodded silently.

"The king is not seeking vengeance, Kore. He is seeking the protection of his people."

"But you have killed so often that you are despised and yet feared. Surely there are not that many who are deserving of death."

"I wish that were true, Kore. If everyone in the kingdom heeded the king's laws, my position would no longer be needed." Justice looked off into the distance, envisioning something Kore could not see. "Someday it will be so. I hope I am here to see it."

"Kore? Are you bringing more wood?" Anna Lea called. "It will take forever to cook this fine chicken over such a tiny flame."

"I'm coming," Kore called back to her. "Have you noticed that she changes?" Kore asked gesturing discreetly toward Anna Lea. "Back at the inn I thought she had lost her mind."

Justice glanced at her, she had skewered the chicken and was dusting the down from her dress. "The madness is an act for her own protection, Kore. There are many men who would take advantage of her if they knew her as she allows us to know her."

Kore looked thoughtfully at Anna Lea.

"Go, she will need the wood if you are to enjoy the meal," Justice prompted wanting to be alone.

Kore headed back to the fire, picking up dry sticks along the way as he went.

Anna Lea watched as Justice rose slowly and placed the letter into the pouch at his side. Once more, he was on a mission to kill. He was not himself. The contents of the letter seemed to weigh heavily on him. The practiced calm she had seen in him before had returned.

When they ate, Justice did not join in their conversation. He was lost in thought, often staring unseeing at the distant horizon. They soon gave up trying to include him. He was stealing himself for the task ahead.

CHAPTER 9

"Wait here, I will return shortly," Justice spoke calmly, as if he were stopping at the house to see a friend.

Neither Kore nor Anna Lea responded as he strode off purposefully along the trail that led to the cottage on the other side of the clearing. When he was half way there, Kore crossed the road and hurried through the thin stand of trees and around the back of the rundown barn.

He drew his breath in sharply when Anna Lea rounded the corner of the barn behind him. "What are you doing here?" he hissed. "Justice said to wait for him back there."

"Is that what you are doing?" Anna Lea asked pointedly.

"Be quiet, I need to see this. I was away when he killed my father, I need to see how it happened."

"I'm coming," Anna Lea answered.

"It is not right for a lady to see…"

"I lived with Wiley Oliver for years, Kore. I have seen men die before."

"Justice won't like it." Kore did not have time to argue. Justice was approaching the door of the cottage. "Fine, but be quiet." He hurried to the side of the cottage and crouched beneath the window. A thin blanket hung over the opening, flapping gently in the afternoon breeze. Standing slowly, Kore pulled back the corner of the blanket. Inside a man was standing, facing Justice. At his side was his young wife, who did not look much older than Anna Lea. She was weeping against the man, pleading for his life. Even from outside, Kore could taste the fear that filled the house.

Justice removed the letter from his pouch and read it aloud. The man had been found guilty of murdering three men in the village they had just passed through. Justice had asked many questions there, confirming the fact that the men were killed, not in self-defense, but for personal-gain.

Justice read the letter in his steady, firm voice, which carried well over the hopeless sobs of the woman. Kore imagined her as his mother, preparing to watch her husband die. Kore could not deny that his father had been a hard, cruel man, but he was now seeing a side of Justice that seemed just as heartless and cold.

Then came the question. "Martin Beckett, did you kill Blair, Dion, and Woodson?"

Martin looked at Justice, meeting his gaze despite the fear that choked him, "No, I did not kill them. Have mercy. I swear, I didn't do it." He fell to his knees and his sobbing wife knelt beside him echoing "Please, have mercy."

Justice said nothing, his face thoughtful as he looked down at them. Martin wore a medium sized hunting knife on his belt. There was no sign of any other weapon, but if he were skilled, the knife would have been enough.

"I swear on the king's throne, I did not kill them," Martin pleaded.

"Who killed them?" Justice was seemingly unmoved by the weeping couple kneeling before him.

Martin looked up, grasping at the faint glimmer of hope. "I don't know. I went into town last week and all three were alive and well. I had a dispute some days before over prices of the furs I brought to him, but I did not kill them. I swear I..."

"Stop swearing everything and think." Justice commanded, jolting the man from his pleading desperation.

Frowning, Martin thought hard. He was very aware

that his life depended on any clue he could remember. "We argued, Woodson and me. He would not buy my furs, and I was forced to go to Thomas. I had to sell him the furs, even though he only paid me a third of what they were worth."

"Why?" Justice interjected.

"My crops were poor this year. The rain did not come, and the earth was too dry. Everyone's crops were lean, but down in the valley, they still had food. We have not had this place long, and things did not grow as we had hoped." He looked down, ashamed, "We had no money for food."

Justice walked to the cupboard and opened the door. There were a few empty canisters inside. Justice took one out and noticed only the tiniest crumbs clung to the bottom of the container. He had passed through the village, and someone could have warned them that he was coming. Remembering the odd mixture of responses from the villagers, Justice weighed the evidence. Only a few of the villagers had been bold about their apparent hatred of the couple on the hill. In Justice's opinion, their complaints had come across as staged and intentional.

Martin and his wife watched him, searching his stoic face for any sign of mercy.

His attention returned to them once more. "Go on."

"I took the money to the market, but no one would sell me anything." Martin's lips quivered with emotion, and he shut them tightly to hide it.

"We were starving," Martin's wife added softly.

"Let him tell it. It is his life at stake," Justice instructed.

"We were starving," Martin repeated. "I was desperate."

"That is the fact and the feeling," Justice was watching Martin intently. "What was the action that followed?"

Martin licked his lips nervously. "I…stole a little loaf of bread when no one was looking." He glanced at his wife, ashamed. "But I left money on the cart to pay for it. It wasn't really stealing."

"It was someone else's bread, and you took it without permission." Justice countered. "Go on."

The hope Martin had felt before was fading quickly, but as it faded, his will to live increased. "Very well, I stole the bread. I brought it back to Sadie." He met Justice's eyes defiantly. "I lied to her and told her I had eaten mine on the way home. She believed me and ate it."

"Oh, Martin," Sadie whispered, starting to cry once more.

"I was desperate. No one would sell to us. We were not wanted, and I could not provide for my wife."

"So you justified stealing and lying. Many desperate men have killed for less."

"But I did not do it. I did not kill those men." Martin stood and faced Justice boldly. "You can kill me, but it was not my hand that took their lives."

Justice smiled slightly. "Thank you. I know it was hard for you, but I have to be sure before I do what I came to do."

"He is telling the truth." Sadie rose with a terrified whimper. "You must believe him," she pleaded.

"I do."

It took them several seconds to comprehend what he had said and the meaning behind it. They stood blinking at him in shock.

"Kore, are you willing to give up your share of remains of the chicken?" Justice stood, unmoving in the center of the bare little cottage.

"Yes." Came the response from the window.

Martin looked around, unable to locate the owner of the voice.

"Anna Lea?" Justice asked, knowing that she too was crouched outside the window.

"Yes, Justice. They may have my share as well."

"I will get it," Kore offered, starting back toward the road.

"There is no need." Justice stepped out of the house and whistled. The sound carried well and it was not long before they heard the quick step of the horse coming their way. It stopped beside Justice and stood ready. It sought no petting or treat for its actions. Obedience itself was the animal's reward. Justice untied the little cloth bundle that held the remains of the cooked chicken and entered the house once more. Sadie was seated, looking faint. Martin stood beside her. Tears of relief streaked his face.

"Thank you, Sir," he said as Justice re-entered their home. "I have never heard of a King's Man sparing the life he was sent to take."

"That is because the order is always received directly from the king himself." Justice laid the bundle of chicken on the table and stepped back. "This letter came from a messenger on the road. A week's time is not enough for word to reach the king and the king to send back his verdict. Death is never commanded without proof of guilt."

"You reflect the king's mercy very well," Martin observed.

Again the slight smile lightened Justice's stoic features.

Martin opened the bundle and unconsciously licked his lips at the sight of food. "You are sure you will not have some?" he asked politely.

When they declined his offer, Martin and Sadie divided what was left of the chicken and ate gratefully.

Justice went to the door and stood looking out over the barren farmland the couple had tried to bring to life. "After you have eaten, you must leave this place," he informed them after several minutes. "The king's soldiers will come and investigate the matter further, but your lives will be in danger if you remain here."

"But where will we go?" Sadie wiped the grease from her fingers with a faded cloth. "We have no money or food."

"We cannot pay the rent on the house," Marin told her.

"What he says is true. Thomas may seek his own justice if we stay."

"But where will we go?" Sadie asked again. Her whole world had been turned upside down.

Anna Lea appeared in the doorway. "Could they not come with us to the Weaver's Refuge?" she asked. "We have no food or money, but we will be safer if we travel together. It will be dark in a few hours."

Martin and Sadie looked at each other. Sadie's eyes traveled around the bare little cottage. She remembered when they had arrived, hopeful and excited about their future together. Now they were leaving it all and fleeing for their lives.

Martin seemed to be sharing her thoughts. He took her hand in his own and knelt beside her. "Wherever we go, you will always be my home."

She smiled at him through her tears, "and you will be mine." She answered with a little sob of a laugh.

They hugged each other tightly.

"We will be outside," Justice informed them, exiting as he spoke.

They rose quickly to pack the few belongings they would need for their journey.

———

"I instructed you to stay by the main road." Justice spoke in a low tone to Kore who walked beside him. "Why did you follow me?"

Kore glanced at their new companions who walked on the other side of the horse, chatting happily with Anna Lea. "I needed to see how the king's justice was carried out."

"How it happened to your father?" Justice clarified, keeping his eyes on the road ahead.

"Yes."

Justice studied the young man beside him, "And were you satisfied?"

"How did you know Martin was innocent? The king's letter said he killed them."

"The letter was not from the king."

Kore stopped in astonishment. "How do you know?"

Anna Lea shot a questioning looked at Kore over the horse's back.

Hurrying to catch up with Justice, Kore asked again in a hushed whisper. "Justice, how did you know the letter was not from the king?"

"I have seen many letters from the king, Kore. I have read them both privately and aloud. Never before have I received a letter of death from the hand of a messenger."

Kore noticed Anna Lea was eaves dropping and shook his head at her. "That is why you sat alone so long when you received it?"

Anna Lea said something to Sadie and slipped around to walk on the far side of Kore.

"We are trying to talk." Kore told her, annoyed.

"It involves her as well. You both disregarded my instructions."

Anna Lea wished at once that she had stayed on the other side of the horse. The disappointment in his voice made her feel like a disobedient child. "I am sorry, Justice, it was not right for us to follow you. I…" she glanced at Kore and fell silent.

Justice stopped walking and faced them, "What I do, and see, is not a show."

They both nodded, thankful the Becketts waited where they were.

"I will give you another chance," Justice said after a pause. "I am returning to the village to find the messenger. You must go on, follow the King's Highway and stick together. Three more days will bring you to the Weaver's Refuge."

"Can we not wait for you here?" Anna Lea asked quickly.

"I will come and help you," Kore offered, and Anna Lea saw Justice's face darken with displeasure.

"You will both go on with the Becketts to the Weaver's Refuge." Justice was untying Anna Lea's bundle from the saddle. He pulled a folded paper from the saddle bag as well. The wax that sealed it bore the imprint of Justice's ring.

"Have you ever let a man live before?" Kore was not happy to be sent away. "I mean before Martin."

"It has happened only this once, but my mission is not yet completed." Justice handed the bundle to Kore and the letter to Martin. "See that you give this to the captain of the guard when you arrive at the Weaver's Refuge. He will know what to do with it."

Martin nodded and tucked the letter safely inside his tunic.

Justice paused to look over the little band. Anna Lea was nervously fiddling with the pleated cloth of her skirt. Kore, with the bundle over his shoulder, looked back dejectedly, hoping Justice would change his mind and take him along. Martin and Sadie stood arm in arm, grateful for each breath together.

"Be wise and travel safely. I would leave the horse to you, but I have need of him. Stick to the highway and travel quickly. There is much evil in these parts."

They stood there, watching silently as Justice turned the horse and mounted. He rode away without looking back.

CHAPTER 10

"Gobi, you should not be here!" Thomas hissed fiercely, slamming the door closed.

"Thomas, let me in. I tell you he is here," Gobi begged though the closed door. "The man from the king is here." He glanced towards the road fearfully.

The door opened and a lean man with a long mustache pulled Gobi inside. Thomas looked Gobi over skeptically, twirling the edge of his mustache with a long fingered hand. "How do you know? No one has ridden into town tonight."

"I saw him on the road. He was riding this way. We must warn the others. If he were to find…"

"Silence!" Thomas hurried to the window and peered out. He saw nothing in the street besides Gobi's mangy gray dog. "So he came back?" Thomas was still twisting his mustache thoughtfully. "Brutus was so sure it would work." He released his mustache and smoothed it reflectively. "If we are careful, we will be able to send him off again without raising suspicion."

Confused, Gobi glanced from Thomas to the door and back again.

"Go to the king's messenger and tell him to keep out of sight. He is the one Justice will be looking for."

Gobi's hand was on the door latch when Thomas added, "And remember, we know nothing about a messenger from the king."

"But Thomas, he was here only a few days ago asking questions. He knows the messenger is here," Gobi protested.

"Was here," Thomas corrected. "He has gone." His eyes were deadly now. "A royal messenger carrying the seal of the king gives us great power. The King's Man must not find him."

Gobi nodded and hurried to obey.

————

"I should go back and help him," Kore muttered, glancing back for what, to the others, felt like the hundredth time.

"You can't help him, Kore," Anna Lea answered firmly. "Stop saying that over and over. You followed him before, and he was not happy about it. Leave him alone, and let him do his job."

Ignoring her, Kore moved to walk beside Martin, asking casually, "What do you think, Martin?"

Martin looked thoughtful, "I don't know. He told us to go on. He just spared my life, so I am inclined to obey."

"And if they kill him?" Kore pressed.

"I don't know, Kore. My life is all shaken up, and his instructions are all I have to go on right now. I have no choice but to trust him and go."

Kore sighed, Martin was not going to give in. "Alright then, we will pick up the pace and do as Justice instructed. But the moment we get there, I'm going to go back for him."

The others made no answer.

————

Turning the horse's head, Justice urged him down the rocky path. The light was almost gone. He had sat there, watching the edge of the village below for almost an hour. He had seen the short, wide man, with a dog trailing behind, scurrying between the houses. It was obvious the informer had caught wind of Justice's approach. The house he had gone to first was the one Justice had watched. It was there that he would find the one who was giving orders to the phony messenger. The king's seal in the hands of a greedy man would cost many an innocent man his life. The horse stumbled and caught itself, jolting Justice in the saddle. Pulling his mount to a stop, Justice dismounted and led it down the boulder strewn path, allowing the animal to find its own footing. It would be dark long before they reached the village. When they came to a portion of the trail that was not as steep, Justice stopped the horse and began removing its saddle and bridle. Running his hand over the clear brand of the king on the horse's flank, Justice stood straighter. He was a King's Man and would not turn from his mission. Draping the reigns over the saddle, Justice carried it back up the path. He could hear the horse cropping away at the withered shrubs that grew between the rocks. There would be no dinner for Justice tonight. He thought briefly of the doctor who had betrayed the king. Did the king really pay the doctor for his service? If so, Justice had been cheated out of his dinner. He touched the cut on his face. It was sore, but not warm to the touch like it had been before. The doctor's medicine must have stayed the infection for now.

The night was coming on quickly as Justice made his way back up to a sheltered outcrop of rock that he had noticed before. He ducked as he entered the makeshift cave made from large boulders which leaned heavily against one another. Even though there were multiple ways in and out of Justice's new camp, not being able to see the sky instantly brought back the terror of being buried alive. He arranged the saddle so he could sleep propped against it, taking his time as he moved pebbles from where he planned to sleep. Prying a loose rock from the ground, he smoothed out the divot where it had been. He paused, the soft dirt under his fingers brought to mind the open grave with chilling clarity. Milo's booming voice rang through his memory, "Get in."

With a forced calm that he did not feel, Justice went to one of the openings and looked out. A gentle breeze blew over him. Closing his eyes, Justice breathed it in gratefully. He thought of the king and the mission at hand allowing the memory to fade. Going back inside, Justice lay down, pillowing his head on the seat of the saddle.

The king had often encouraged Justice to take along a companion for protection along the way. Until now, a companion had seemed like an unnecessary burden that would only slow him down. But tonight, as he lay on the hard ground, Justice wondered how the others were faring. Had Anna Lea convinced Kore to follow his instructions? Justice rolled to his side. He was surprised to find he missed their companionship.

———

"I am here to speak to the messenger from the king." Justice guided his mount to the center of the main street. It intrigued him that not one villager stopped to answer him or even acknowledged his presence. They scurried past like ants heading back to their nest. A lean man with a long mustache emerged from one of the houses, and Justice rode towards him. "I am here to speak to the messenger from the king."

"He is no longer here." Thomas twisted his mustache and studied the King's Man before him. "I believe he had already delivered his message."

Justice could see the lean man knew more than he let

on. "You are a man of authority here. What is your name?"

"Thomas Jacobs." He spoke his name as if it were a challenge, but Justice had not heard it before and went on with his questioning.

"You are responsible to the king for this village?" Justice asked.

Thomas's mustache rose with his smile, "You might say that."

Justice's face displayed no emotion. "And you are sure the messenger has gone? When did he leave?"

Thomas looked thoughtfully at his long fingers. "He stopped for a meal here after he had delivered his message and then headed back to the road. I can only guess he was headed back to the palace. He was not the talkative type."

"He would fit in quite well here," Justice observed, as a mother hurried by with a child in tow and her eyes on the ground.

"It is market day. The people are getting their food for the week," Thomas explained. "Rain has been scarce and the food shortage is a great concern."

"Very well. If," Justice emphasized the word, "he has already gone. I wish to see the graves of the three men who were killed."

Thomas blinked at Justice. He had not anticipated the request, and thus had not planned his answer.

Justice dismounted and caught the arm of a passing man. The man carried two baskets of scrawny produce.

"If you will excuse me, I must get to market to set up my booth. I am late already, and people will be waiting." The man did not raise his eyes from the ground.

"I have only one question, and then you are free to go," Justice informed him.

The man glanced at Thomas before meeting Justice's eyes expectantly.

"Where are the three men buried who were killed last week."

Again the man's eyes darted to Thomas for a brief instant, "I...I don't know."

"Three men from this village were killed, were they not?" Justice looked from the farmer to Thomas.

"Yes," Thomas responded, knowing Justice already knew the answer.

"And, I assume that someone here buried them, since over a week has passed and they are not lying around anywhere I can see. Is this true?"

Another glance at Thomas, and the farmer managed a hesitant, "Yes."

"Good," Justice met the lean man's hard eyes. "Then I will ask you again. Where were they buried?"

"Outside of town," the farmer stammered, not noticing that Justice was not asking him. Sidestepping Justice, he hurried off down the street.

"Strange that your people have such bad memories," Justice observed with a chilling calm. "Perhaps you can take me to the graves. Unless you too have forgotten."

Thomas glowered darkly but did not dare protest. He called to a man across the street who started towards them at once.

"You will show me the graves." Justice's eyes had not left Thomas's.

Thomas waved the man away once more and straightened his shirt in with a lofty, irritated manner. "If you insist." He stalked down the street. He was heading toward the house Justice had observed from the mountain the night before.

As he followed, Justice thoughtfully fingered the reigns he held. If the three men were killed near this man's house, it would make sense that they would also be buried there to avoid drawing extra attention to the event. Perhaps the three men had been loyal to the king and refused to submit to Thomas's rise in power. Justice would need a way to find out who these men were and why they were killed. The king's letter had been skillfully forged, but Justice was there to see that the punishment for the murders was carried out.

CHAPTER 11

"So, Anna Lea, where did you grow up?" Sadie was stirring the roots and herbs she had found along the road into a makeshift, watery soup. The small pot had come from Anna Lea's little bundle, and for once, Kore was grateful to have it along.

Anna Lea was aware, without looking his way, that Kore had stopped what he was doing to listen.

Leaning over the pot to add the last handful of the root she had been chopping, Anna Lea smiled at the fragrant soup. "This smells delicious, Sadie! You will have to teach me what is safe to eat as we travel. With two more days ahead and not a coin between us, we are going to need to make more of this."

They chatted together about the various herbs until Sadie declared the soup to be done.

Anna Lea sat back on her heels and looked at Sadie in dismay. "How do we eat it? We have no containers or utensils."

"Never fear, kind lady." Kore rose, and with a flourishing bow, he presented her with four crudely carved wooden spoons.

"Kore," her eyes shone with amazement. "I didn't know you could make things like this!" She turned the spoons this way and that as she admired them.

"Well, don't lick them or you will probably get a splinter in your tongue, but they will do the job." Kore was fairly glowing with pride, though he tried to downplay his accomplishment.

Martin grinned past them at Sadie, enjoying their excitement. Her eyes lit up with silent laughter, and she smiled back at him. Martin suddenly realized that they had not laughed together in months. They had no food, or shelter, but the encounter with Justice had given them their life back. They were still young and could start again together. Sadie saw the hope dawn in his expression and was thankful.

"And, if the ladies would gather here at our fine dining table…" Martin gestured grandly at the flat rock beside him. While they were cooking, Martin had cut open two dried gourds and cleaned them out with his knife. Though the resulting bowls were uneven and tipped easily, they were what was needed. Anna Lea and Sadie admired them with laughter as they arranged themselves around the low flat rock he had chosen.

Using a portion of her skirt, Sadie took the little pot by its handle and brought it to them, as if it were a grand feast. And so it was, because it was the first they had eaten that day.

There was not enough soup for the group to eat their fill, but each received enough to quench the pangs of hunger.

Kore drank the last of the broth from his bowl and sighed. "I believe that is the best soup I've tasted this week!"

The others laughed, knowing it was also the only soup he had tasted.

"Anna Lea," Kore looked at her, and she knew what was coming before he asked.

"I will clean up the pot," she said rising quickly.

"Kore and I will clean the dishes," Martin offered with a grin at Kore. "You ladies did the cooking. But you are right, the sun is climbing fast, and we must be on our way."

"You never answered Sadie's question earlier." Kore had not moved from his place. "We would like to hear where you grew up for we know very little about one another." He could see his statement made her uncomfortable. Gathering the makeshift dishes, he added "We will have plenty of time for stories on the road. I will ask you then."

———

"And you say the men had no family?" Justice looked at the unmarked graves. The dirt was settling as time passed, and it would not be long before the graves disappeared completely. "That is why you have not marked them."

"There was no need. These men were," Thomas paused, considering his words carefully. "They were quiet men with no connections to anyone. They came to our village, simply living their lives here among us. When Martin killed them, it was a shock to us all."

"Why did he kill them," Justice had noticed a single flower on the center grave. It was wilting, but had been placed there early that morning or sometime in the night. Someone did care about this man.

Thomas thought for a moment before responding. He knew his stories must match if he hoped to be rid of Justice. "One of them would not sell him something at the market. I was told that the item was promised to someone else, but Martin flew into a rage. Later that evening, he found them together and killed them."

"All three of them?" Justice asked cocking an eyebrow.

"I was not there when it happened," Thomas reminded him coolly.

"So Martin, upset about the item, presumably food that he could not buy at the market, found the man who would not sell it to him and killed him?"

"Yes."

"You said it happened that evening?"

Hesitating, Thomas nodded.

"But why did he kill the other two?" Justice asked, looking over the graves thoughtfully.

"They must have tried to save Woodson. Martin was a crazed man and would do anything to get even. He had all kinds of notions about the villagers trying to run him off and even kill him." Thomas looked sad. "His crops did very poorly this year, and many think it did something to his mind."

Justice did not take the new trail of conversation offered by Thomas. "Let me see if I have your story straight."

"My story!" Thomas interjected with irritation. His right hand went to his belt, but he caught himself and casually hooked his thumb into the strap of leather. In his burst of passion, Thomas had forgotten he was not wearing his sword. Justice noted the motion without comment.

Thomas spoke with a forced calm. "It is not my story. It is the facts."

"The facts then," Justice went on casually, "are that Martin, believing he was wronged, approached Woodson that evening with the intent to do him harm. Then, in the evening light, he managed to overpower and kill all three of them without an alarm being raised. No one heard them shout for help or came running at the sound of the fight?"

Thomas faltered for a moment.

"You live there, in that house, do you not?" Justice pointed to the house. He had seen Thomas emerge from it that morning from his camp on the mountain.

Again, Thomas looked surprised, "I..."

"It is best to answer truly. There are many facts I have already discovered on my own." Justice's tone was threatening. "Do you live there?"

"Of course, it is my house," Thomas was twisting one end of his mustache, giving it a lopsided look.

"Did you not hear the commotion as they fought together?"

"I was not at home that night." Thomas regretted his admission immediately.

Justice stooped and took a handful of the dirt from the third man's grave, "Where were you?"

Trapped, Thomas searched for an answer that would satisfy the King's Man. If only he had his sword, he could have made quick work of the assassin crouched before him.

Standing once more, Justice let the dirt trail from his hand as he spoke. "Your account does not make sense, Thomas. One wiry young farmer killing three armed men inside your village before the sun had set without anyone stepping in to help? Yes, I know they were armed. I learned that on my last visit. Surely you see that there are some important facts missing."

"Have you never fought and killed more than one man before?"

"I have not," Justice answered, enjoying the surprised look Thomas gave him.

Thomas recovered himself and jeered. "They defeated you then?" He laughed cruelly. "Your face bears the evidence."

"I believe you know better than that." Justice let the thought sink in before turning back to the unmarked graves. It is customary for graves to be marked. As a leader in this village, you would have been present when they were laid to rest. Who is in each grave?" It was the center grave, the one with the flower, that Justice needed to know. Someone cared about that man's death. If Justice found out who it was, he was sure they would lead him to the killer.

"I do not have time to attend the funerals of common villagers." Thomas' pride flared. "Their graves are there. You have seen them. Now, you may leave our village."

Justice met Thomas' glare with an eerie calm, "I am here, summoned by the king's seal, for the killer of these men. I do not intend to leave until I have completed my mission."

CHAPTER 12

"I'll take these back and pack them up," Martin rose, the homemade dishes were piled into the small cooking pot, and the freshly filled canteen was slung across his chest. As he started up the rise, he paused and looked at Kore with a grin. "It would not hurt to splash a bit of that water on your face."

"What?" Kore tried to look at his reflection in the water. The tiny stream, gurgling around and over the rocks offered no reflection besides that of the sun.

"You are covered in dust, Kore," Martin laughed. "That is why Anna Lea smiles at you the way she does, and why she would not tell you what amused her."

Kore rubbed a wet hand against his cheek and looked at it. A thin layer of mud on his hand confirmed Martin's observance.

"Why did you not tell me before?" Kore asked, annoyed at Anna Lea and the others.

"There was nothing you could do about it then. The canteen was low." Still grinning, Marten crested the rise and was soon out of sight.

"They could have told me," Kore muttered, splashing and rubbing his face vigorously. Since Justice had sent them away, Kore had somehow felt the others were to blame. Taking off his shirt, he shook it violently to knock off the layer of dust from the road. He slipped it back on and once more muddied the little stream as he washed his face and hair. Kore was thoroughly involved in his task and did not notice the two men who approached from the other side of the little stream.

"Rats here says you double-crossed us." Milo's voice sent Kore scrambling to his feet. He stared at them, dripping and wide eyed. "What are you doing here?" he demanded, keeping his voice low so that the others would not hear over the little ridge that separated them.

"I don't take kindly to people who cross me," Milo informed Kore darkly.

Beside Milo stood Rats, as fidgety and repulsing as ever. He grinned at Kore, his teeth rotted and yellow beneath his scrawny mustache.

"I did not cross you, Milo." Kore glanced back once more towards their camp to insure no one was watching. "Justice dug his way out. I don't know how he did it. The only thing I dug up was his sword, and that was after he was out."

"I don't believe you." Milo's eyes were hard.

"That is what happened, Milo. I swear I did not help him out of that grave." Kore searched for a way to prove it. His eyes lit up, "His face. Did Rats tell you about Justice's face too, or just that he was alive?"

Milo glanced at Rats who was eager to share all he knew. "He's got a big gash, right down the side of his face now." Tracing the line of Justice's wound on his own face. "Looked bad, but I heard the doctor treated him.

"What does this wound prove?" Milo demanded.

"He was not injured as badly as you thought when you stabbed his sword into the grave." Kore met Milo's eyes. "You almost missed him completely. A scratch isn't going to keep someone like Justice down for long."

The edge of the big man's mouth turned up into a cruel smile. "So I gave it to him? I see now that I should have been more thorough. You say you did not help him, but you are helping him now. Brutus told us you are traveling with him."

"That is my business," Kore answered with a boldness he did not feel. "I never joined your band. You know that. I went along to watch, nothing more."

"Is that what you told him?" Milo asked with a short laugh. "You have more cleverness than I gave you credit for. So he believed you and took you along."

Kore shrugged, "Something like that."

Nodding, Milo looked at Kore, seeming to read something deeper in the young man. "Yes, perhaps it is for the best. Without him, we would not have her."

Seeing Kore's confused frown, Milo nudged Rats, knocking the thin man off balance. "You see that, Rats. The King's Man was planning on keeping the reward to himself."

"What reward?" Kore knew the others would be looking for him soon.

"And he sent you on alone. To deliver her to the king. All the time planning on collecting the reward himself."

"I don't know what you are talking about," Kore insisted.

"Did the Assassin give you a letter to deliver at your destination?" Milo asked, casually brushing something invisible from his sleeve.

Kore thought for a moment. "He gave a letter to Martin."

"Maybe he doesn't trust you," Milo pointed out. "The girl you are traveling with is the only daughter of Counselor and Lady Hillcrest. Their entire estate passes to her in the event of their death."

Kore stared at them blankly.

"They are dead, Kore. Killed nearly three years ago by Wiley Oliver, the man I was told you helped to bury."

"Anna Lea?" Kore was struggling to comprehend it all.

"I believe her full title is Annalise Leona Hillcrest." Milo stepped across the stream and grabbed the front of Kore's shirt. "I want that reward."

Kore pushed Milo's hand from his shirt and scrambled out of reach. "No, Justice knew nothing of this. He would not let her travel with him. He only gave in because we needed protection on the road at night."

"Intriguing how such a man can guide the minds of simple folk so that they do his will unknowingly."

"Kore, are you coming?" Martin called from the top of the rise. "You only had to wash your face, man. Make haste, the daylight will not wait for you."

"I am coming," Kore called back.

Martin stood there a minute more, sizing up the men talking with Kore down below. Even from a distance, Kore could read the distrust in his companion's manner.

"We are coming, too," Milo informed him. "I am a fair man, Kore. You brought her this far and have won her trust. We will travel with you and split the reward."

When Kore hesitated, Milo stepped closer, "We travel with you, or we take the girl."

Kore glanced up the rise helplessly, but said nothing when they followed him up to join the others.

By the time they reached the top, Kore had control of himself once more. "Sorry to delay you so long." He called cheerily. "I ran into some acquaintances who are traveling our way. I thought we could use a few members in our band who are not as poor as church mice."

Rats looked uncomfortable, but Milo laughed and greeted the others cheerily. The big man could see the others did not trust him, but they had no choice in the matter. Shouldering Anna Lea's bundle, Kore led their band back to the King's Highway.

————

"Excuse me?"

The man turned, but when he saw Justice, he dropped his eyes and attempted to hurry past.

Justice grabbed the man's arm and spun him so that they were face to face.

"Our town has rules about that type of treatment," the villager protested angrily.

"Besides the king's rules?" Justice tapped the underside of his ring on the hilt of his sword. Both bore the clear insignia of the king.

The villager scowled at the ground.

"I have only one question for you. It is a very simple question that a child could easily answer."

Knowing he would not be permitted to leave without answering, the villager raised his gaze to the face of the King's Man.

"Did Martin carry a sword when he came into town?"

The man's attention flicked momentarily to something behind Justice, and his expression changed slightly. "No, he always carried a hunting knife, but nothing more."

Justice stooped to pick up a small stone from the ground. As he did so, he glanced in the direction the villager had looked. There, leaning against the side of a house, was the short, wide man fondling the ears of his gray dog. Rising, Justice tossed the stone upward and caught it easily.

When their eyes met again, there was a knowing in the face of both men. The conversation they had would be carried to the ears of another.

"How long was the knife?" Justice was still toying with the stone.

"You said one question, and I answered you." The villager was moving away from Justice.

"It is true. You are free to go."

The villager paused, unsure if the polite dismissal was

intended to be obeyed. Seeing no objection from Justice, he hurried off, only to be called over by the short, wide man. "Did you have a good conversation, Hadly?"

Hadly looked back to make sure the King's Man was not coming their way. "Gobi, I had no choice. I did not tell him anything he does not already know."

"What did he ask you?" Gobi was fondling the dog's ears once more.

"Could you not hear?" Hadly asked, knowing he was taking a chance.

Gobi did not look up, "Thomas will not be happy to hear of your insubordinate tongue."

"I told him Martin carried a knife," Hadly informed him. "He asked me directly, and that was all the information I gave." Gobi stood suddenly and Hadly followed his gaze. Thomas Jacobs was coming their way.

"Hadly was chatting with the king's assassin," Gobi told him as he approached. "It seems he does not appreciate your protection."

"What did you talk about?" Thomas asked.

"He asked if Martin carried a sword. I was going to ignore him and walk by, but he grabbed my arm. I am not going to fight the king's assassin. I have heard the fate of those who do." Hadly was irritated at being detained once more for questioning. "No one speaking to him is only making him more suspicious."

"I will decide that. What did you say to him?" Thomas asked, his tone firm.

"I told him Martin only carried a hunting knife. The King's Man would have seen the knife when he went to kill Martin," Hadly pointed out. "He would have known if I lied to him."

"I see no harm was done. Keep away from him. He has gleaned some information from you and may try to get more."

Hadly nodded. "I went up to Martin's place this morning."

"Oh?"

"Sadie is gone. The house is empty."

"That was sudden. Where would she go?" Gobi inquired.

"What did she have to keep her here?" Hadly asked in return.

"Thank you for the report, Hadly. You may go."

Smiling to himself, Hadly hurried away. He had not told them that he had looked around and had found no grave. Perhaps the inquisitive assassin knew more than he let on.

CHAPTER 13

"Kore, I do not like these men," Anna Lea whispered, handing him the canteen she had brought from Martin. Their band no longer walked closely together, as if each sought to distance him or herself from the newcomers.

"They have money." Kore took a swig from the canteen and handed it back to her. "We need that right now." He looked at her trying to imagine her as a lady with a grand estate. Anna Lea had been silent since Milo and Rats had joined their band. Kore wondered if she would pretend madness if forced to speak, and for that reason, had not attempted to draw her out. It would not matter. The reward was for her return. If she chose to act mad, it would only make it easier for them to give her up.

"Why are you staring at me?" she asked uneasily.

Kore changed the subject. "You never answered Sadie's question from lunch. I am very interested in your answer."

She frowned and searched his eyes for the reason for this sudden interest. Was there something he knew? Something those terrible men had told him?

"We could all use a good story right now." Kore had raised his voice so the others could hear.

"Then why don't you tell them all about your father?" Anna Lea turned away and hurried to catch up with Sadie and Martin who walked ahead.

———

"I told you not to come here," Thomas observed coldly.

"No one saw me come," Gobi pointed out. "Justice left town almost an hour ago." He grinned. "No one would give him a place for the night. The villagers fear you too much to cross you."

"Yes, they obey me, but you do not. I do not want you coming here."

"It is important," Gobi whined.

Thomas rolled his eyes, "Come in."

Gobi followed him into the little cottage. Thomas took his place at the table and returned to his dinner without offering Gobi a seat.

"Justice has been asking questions all over town. He makes each person answer just one question."

"And they answer him?" Thomas asked darkly.

"What choice do they have? He is a King's Man bearing the king's emblem. If they were not loyal to the king, his messenger would be worthless."

"You think too much, Gobi," Thomas informed him. "Who has he questioned?"

"Nearly everyone on this side of the village. Men, women, children, but never the same person twice. I'll give him that. He is true to his word and only requires one answer."

"And the messenger?" Thomas asked.

"He is unhappy about being kept inside." Gobi inched closer to the table. "Sure smells good."

Thomas ignored the hint from Gobi. "Has he finished the letter as I directed?"

"Yes, I instructed him not to seal it until you have time to look it over."

"Good. Tomorrow morning, you will keep an eye on the

Assassin so that I can go to the messenger unseen."

"Yes, I will do that," Gobi agreed as if he had a choice.

"Justice said he was here to carry out the instructions of the king's letter." Thomas twisted his mustache thoughtfully. "At the time, I assumed he believed the letter was from the king. But he should have already killed Martin by then." Thomas rose threateningly from his seat. "Is Martin dead?"

"Hadly said earlier that he had gone to the house. Remember, he said that Sadie has gone and the house is empty. Why would she go if Martin was still alive? You know that they were determined to stay there even when we tried to starve them out."

"Yes," Thomas sat as his mind churned the new information. Something was not adding up. "Tomorrow, you will go up and check the house yourself. Hadly was a friend of Martin's, and he may be trying to buy Martin time to escape."

"You said I was to keep an eye on Justice," Gobi pointed out. He dreaded the long hot walk to the Beckett place.

"I will send someone else then. That is all for tonight."

Gobi lingered, looking longingly at the cooked pheasant Thomas was carving.

"Was there something else?" Thomas inquired.

"No, Sir." Gobi went to the door and stepped out. The darkness enveloped him, and he waited for his eyes to adjust. He thought he saw movement in the direction of the graves, but the gray dog made no sound to indicate an intruder. The dog got up sleepily and walked beside Gobi as he crossed the street and headed home.

————

Justice stood still, waiting without a sound until Gobi was gone. The drugged meat had silenced Gobi's dog, freeing

Justice to listen. Thomas suspected him, and Justice knew he did not have much time. He would have to find the murderer and bring him, and the traitorous messenger back to the king for judgment. Tomorrow, Thomas would lead him to the messenger. It would be two more days before his letter for reinforcements would reach the guard at the Weaver's Refuge, and at least two more, if they rode hard, for the soldiers to reach him.

Justice moved away from the house to sit by a boulder on the far side of the graves. The rock would make his silhouette less noticeable. His stomach growled, and he wished he had kept part of the rat he had fed to the dog to keep it quiet. He had no money to buy food and better understood Martin's desperation when his crops had failed. The villagers feared Thomas enough to turn away from the needs of their own people.

Leaning back against the rock, Justice waited. His eyes were closed, but he heard every sound. Several hours passed. The lamp in Thomas' house was blown out, and the village grew still. Above, the waxing moon shone dimly on the three humps of earth. Three lives taken, and for what purpose?

Justice was aware of soft footsteps long before he saw the woman. Her features were hidden by the shawl she wore over her head and shoulders as she crept towards the graves. She paused in the shadows, looking keenly around as if aware she was being watched. Justice diverted his eyes, but watched her still. She crossed the open space and knelt by the center grave. Placing at its head a single flower, she gently laid her hand on the mound of earth which covered the man she loved.

Justice waited, allowing her to grieve alone. She had lost much, and Justice knew the pain such a loss could bring. She rose, and the tears on her cheeks glistened in the pale moonlight.

"What was his name?" Justice asked softly.

She gasped, clapping a hand over her mouth to keep from screaming. She stood as if frozen with her back to Justice.

The silence stretched on as Justice waited. Finally, when Justice had almost given up hope, he heard her whispered reply.

"Woodson." Her voice was barely audible and choked with sadness.

"Thank you."

She turned, searching the darkness for the source of the voice. Justice was still, waiting.

"Martin did not kill my brother."

"Who then?" He wanted to rush to her, to beg her for the answer, but he remained hidden in the shadow of the rock.

A twig snapped, and she fled, disappearing like a phantom into the dark shadows.

Justice did not try to follow. He was one tiny step closer to the truth.

CHAPTER 14

"Where is she?!" Milo demanded angrily, scrambling to his feet.

"Who?" Martin's voice was thick with sleep.

"Annalise! Where is she?!" He bellowed, searching for any sign of where she had gone.

"Annalise?" Sadie asked with a confused frown.

"He means Anna Lea," answered Kore, not bothering to roll over to face them. "He's not good with names." The sky was a pale gray in anticipation of the sun's first rays.

"Get up, all of you!" Milo ordered, his voice threatening.

At that moment, Anna Lea came into the camp from the narrow trail that led to the stream they had discovered the night before. Her face, still rosy from the cold water, paled when she caught sight of Milo's scowl. She looked at Martin and Sadie for an explanation. They stood together, looking confused and sleepy. Her eyes moved to Kore who had not risen with the others. Fear washed over her, Milo's hateful look made her feel vulnerable and alone. How she wished for the protecting presence of Justice.

"Where were you?" Milo demanded.

Anna Lea suddenly giggled. "Were you all waiting for me?"

Another giggle and Kore groaned, pulling his blanket over his head.

"You all look so bedraggled." A tittering laugh escaped her before her explanation. "I had to wash my face. Imagine, you all ready to leave so early and my down there washing." Her giggle got out of control and almost turned into the hideous laugh she'd used at the inn.

Kore rolled and glared at her. "Don't! You have made enough noise already."

"So you can talk." Rats rubbed his twitching nose. "I had begun to think you couldn't."

Anna Lea suppressed another giggle. "Of course I can! But someone told me I talk too much and to be quiet." She looked meaningfully at Kore, but he could see that in her mind she was reliving a different memory. She flinched and caught herself, covering with the annoying giggle. This time, it was hollow and dry.

Milo, angry to have made such a display, was rolling up his blanket, ignoring Anna Lea completely.

"Well," Anna Lea looked around, her fresh giggle ending in a little snort. "If you don't mind if I talk…"

"We do mind," Kore interrupted. "Be quiet." He glanced over at the Becketts who had shown no sign of surprise at Anna Lea's strange behavior.

Anna Lea gave him a patronizing little smile and picked up her blanket. Kore, who was down wind, was showered with dirt.

He scrambled to his feet with an angry shout. Warning looks from both Milo and Martin sent him muttering back to gather his blanket.

They packed up in silence. Anna Lea's blanket went into her bundle, while the rest of them carried their own.

After his outburst, Anna Lea had not spoken again. Kore watched her discreetly as they waited for Martin and Sadie to return from filling the canteens at the spring. She had never spoken to them of her parents and had endured much since their deaths. Yet she had found a way to cope, and had dared to trust again.

Kore hated himself for what he was doing to her. She had trusted him, laying aside her silly front and allowing him to see her for who she was. Or, Kore told himself, who she wanted them to see. If it were true that she was the heir to a great estate, all she had been was a lie. Moody and silent, Kore sat alone. He had allowed life to happen, going along with whatever whim caught his eye. He had watched without protest as Milo drove the sword into Justice's grave. Then, not long after, had dug up that same sword for the man it was intended to kill. Now, Kore had not only broken her trust, but he had put Anna Lea into grave danger.

"We will start early since we are all up," Milo announced when the Becketts had returned. No one protested. He turned to Anna Lea. "Don't ever leave camp without my permission," he commanded darkly.

"Something terrible could happen to you out there," Rats agreed. He did not have the imposing presence of a big man like Milo and knew better the value of keeping the peace.

Kore got to his feet, carefully avoiding the questioning looks Martin and Sadie gave him. They started off without breakfast. Milo and Rats had dried beef in their pouches, but did not offer it to the others. Kore was in a sour mood. Having money did them little good, when there was no inn or village to buy food.

———

Justice waited, hidden out of sight beyond the graves. He was watching Thomas' door. Today he would go to the messenger. If Justice could find him, half of the job would be done.

The sky grew pale and still there was no movement from the house. The sun crested the horizon. Its brilliant rays cast long shadows across the empty streets.

The door opened, and Thomas checked the street. Slipping out, he turned a key in the door before striding quickly across to the shadow of the nearest house. Again and again, he checked the street before moving to the next shadow. Justice moved in, falling easily into the lean man's predictable pattern. Staying a house or two behind Thomas, Justice made his way to a rundown place on the outskirts of the village. The thatched roof was falling, crumbling in a couple of places, and the door hung lazily from one strap.

Justice crouched and watched. He had no fear of being discovered by Gobi. He had seen him and his dog sitting vigilantly by the road Justice used to enter the village each morning. Having taken his horse up to the mountain the night before, Justice had circled around to spend the night at the graveside. And so, Gobi sat watching vainly for the return of the King's Man.

Thomas looked around. The sun's rays were stronger and the shadows were losing their inky blackness. Drawing back, Justice held his breath. His stomach growled loudly, and Justice chided himself for not dealing with that issue before now.

Seeing nothing amiss, Thomas slipped through the crooked door, disappearing inside. Justice rose and circled the house. Finding a tree a little ways behind the house, he leaned casually against it and watched as the villagers started emerging sleepily from their houses to go to work in their fields. The women or older children went to the well for water, each attending to their own task. Some chatted cheerfully as they waited for their turn to draw water. This was a side of the village Justice had not seen. They were held down by Thomas Jacob's narrow thumb, but they had not lost their will to thrive.

Thomas emerged and looked around. He wore a satisfied

smile, apparently pleased by the work of the messenger. Moving quickly, he distanced himself from the rundown structure before starting back towards his own house. When he was out of sight, Justice walked purposefully to the door Thomas had just emerged from. Slipping inside, he looked around. It was a bare room, completely void of any sign of life. Except... Justice crouched and examined the floor. Thomas had left a trail to the cellar door through the layer of dust that coated the floor.

———

They traveled for almost an hour before Kore managed to maneuver himself unnoticed to Martin's side. He walked alone, allowing Sadie, her arm linked with Anna Lea's, to offer her the silent comfort of companionship. Walking a few paces behind them, Martin watched their band with a wary look.

"Martin," Kore glanced back at Milo who was having an intense conversation with Rats. The big man seemed to have forgotten them. It would be safe to talk. "Do you still have that letter Justice gave you before he left?"

"Yes?" Martin's answer was guarded. He shifted the bundle to his opposite shoulder so he could see Kore better.

"What does it say?"

Martin turned to look at Kore, shocked by the question. "I do not read the private messages others have entrusted to me."

"I know," Kore kept his voice low. "But what if the letter instructs the soldiers to arrest us or even execute us? All I am saying is that we do not know if delivering it will bring us harm."

"You do not know him well, do you?" Martin pitied the

young man beside him.

"Justice? No, I've only known him for a few days at most," answered Kore defensively.

"Wasn't that enough time for you to see the kind of man that he is?"

Kore walked in silence. He was betraying Justice by betraying Anna Lea, but Justice was gone, and Milo and Rats were both dangerous men if they were crossed. Kore told himself he had no choice. They would give her to the soldiers at the Weaver's Refuge. She would be safe there. They would collect their reward, and be on their way. Kore thought of the big meal he would buy with his share of the reward.

Martin interrupted his thoughts. "Anna Lea needs your help."

Looking ahead, Kore noticed nothing amiss.

"She needs to be able to trust you," Martin went on. "I do not know why you have brought these men, perhaps you had no choice, but she needs you to stand for her."

"What are you two jabbering about up there?" Milo demanded. The closer they got to the Weaver's Refuge, the more Milo seemed to take charge of their little band. He was harsh and demanding. Though no one appreciated his company, they dared not cross him.

Martin stopped and faced Milo, "I would like to stop to eat."

"And what would you eat?" Milo sneered.

"The path is lined with herbs and roots that are edible. We had no supper last night, and we could travel more quickly if we had food."

"We don't have time to stop," Milo growled.

"You have food of your own, and unless you are willing to share it with the ladies, I must insist that we stop to eat."

Milo towered over Martin, his eyes hard. "I say we are not stopping."

"Then you can travel on…"

Milo struck Martin, knocking him to the ground. Sadie gave a little cry, but did not move from Anna Lea's side. She could feel her companion trembling.

"Stop that," Kore stood between them. "You joined our band, not the other way around." He saw Milo's eyes drift to Anna Lea. "We are stopping to eat. If you don't like it, you can do as Martin suggested and walk on."

They waited tensely as Milo considered his options. "Rats will go ahead as a scout, and we will join him after the meal." Milo decided. Rats went begrudgingly. Kore had heard it mentioned when they were arguing before. Apparently Rats had lost the argument.

Kore offered Martin his hand, pulling him his feet. Wiping the blood from the side of his mouth, Martin eyed Milo, as if sizing him up.

"Let it go," Kore warned. "He is not one to cross."

The meal was nothing like their last, jolly affair. They worked in silence, gathering the herbs and roots they could use. Martin chopped them deftly with his hunting knife, keeping an eye on Milo as he worked. Kore returned from the stream several minutes later, informing them that water was a good way from the road now and that they would have to be more careful with the supply they carried in their canteens. They had only two between them all. The one brought along by Anna Lea had belonged to the late Wiley Oliver. The other, was used by Milo alone. Rats used a thin metal bottle that he had taken with him up the road.

Martin divided the broth between them once the soup was done. Anna Lea shook her head when he came to her. Martin frowned and took her gourd. It had been damaged along the road and was badly cracked. "Have mine," Martin offered, taking it from Sadie who had been holding it upright. "I will use the pan."

Anna Lea accepted it with a grateful look. Before, the proceedings would have been accompanied by laughter and fun, but Milo's presence was a foreboding one, and there was not so much as a smile among them. Using one of the spoons, Martin divided the cooked, sliced roots between the bowls, leaving a portion for himself in the pan. They ate quickly without speaking to one another."

Milo scowled at them as they ate. They had not shared or even offered their meager meal.

"Alright, you have eaten. Let's go."

When Martin mentioned cleaning their dishes, Milo shook his head. "You bring them as they are or leave them behind. We will not waste any more time."

The soup had been mostly water, so they wrapped the dishes in a blanket, tied up the bundle, and returned to the road. The pangs of hunger had been replaced by pangs of dread. Rats had gone ahead, which could only mean trouble would be waiting when they arrived.

CHAPTER 15

Thomas grabbed the messenger, propelling him into a secluded area behind the booths of the sellers. "What are you doing here?" Thomas demanded, checking to make sure they had not been followed.

"He has the king's seal."

Thomas's face darkened with rage.

"He followed you this morning and came in not long after you left." The messenger was talking fast, "I was sealing the letter for his death sentence as you requested, when he grabbed the seal from my hand." The traitorous messenger did not care what happened to Thomas, or the villagers now. He had known from the beginning that forging letters in the king's name, using the seal of the king to mislead and bring false judgment, was punishable by death. However, when he saw Justice's hand close over the seal, he knew he did not have long to live.

"How did you get away?" Thomas glanced around for any sign of Justice. The messenger could have easily betrayed Thomas to gain his own freedom.

"He tied me up, but left me in the cellar," the messenger scoffed. "He intends to arrest you and bring us both to the king. I cut the rope with the glass of a broken jar."

"Did you mention me?" Thomas watched the man for any sign of betrayal.

"Of course not," the messenger answered hotly. "What

do you take me for, a simpleton?"

"Calm down," Thomas frowned and stroked his mustache. "Justice left you unguarded. That means he must feel very confident in his evidence. We must get the seal back. You will write another letter."

The messenger cocked his head, trying to follow the logic.

"He has the seal, does he not?" Thomas pointed out, putting his hand on the messenger's shoulder. "We will frame him, prove he has misused the seal, and kill him as is the rightful punishment."

Smiling, the messenger removed Thomas' hand. "You are very confident, Thomas, perhaps too confident. I will write the letter and give you until sundown to have the King's Man in your possession. If all goes well, I will testify against him, accusing him of holding me against my will and using my supplies for his own gain." The messenger paused before adding, "If he evades you, I will flee for my life. Without the seal, we have no power over these people."

"Don't worry. I have a plan," Thomas' smile was that of a deadly serpent.

———

Justice walked through the market, scanning the crowds for Thomas. As he approached, the villagers fell silent, waiting until he was several feet away before they rejoined their subdued bartering. It was market day again, and the villagers crowded into the paths between the booths to select the produce they could afford.

The tantalizing smells that drifted on the wind, pulled Justice's attention from his mission. He breathed in deeply and his stomach growled in response. He was hungry and had been for days. Since he had arrived, Justice had been living on the meager meat of the groundhog-like mountain creatures and the tasteless roots he managed to pry from the rocky crevices.

A lady approached Justice, looking furtively around. Justice watched her quizzically. It was broad daylight, and yet she acted as if her actions would not be seen by the others crowding around the booths. She approached him, still looking about and drawing more attention than she was avoiding.

"It isn't right. You are here to help us. We should be helping you." She held out a folded cloth with something inside. When he did not take it, she put it into his hand and scurried away. Justice looked around to see if any of the onlookers understood her strange behavior. They diverted their attention and turned back to their shopping.

Moving out of the throng, Justice found a quiet place to examine the gift. Inside the cloth was a warm meat pastry. The shell was fresh and flakey, and he could smell the rich meat hidden inside.

Biting into the pastry, Justice sighed. It was delicious!

He left the market and headed towards Thomas' house. He had the messenger and needed only the man behind him. The tid-bits of information he had gleaned from the villagers made a patchy story with very little facts. He had needed a solid piece of evidence to convict Thomas and the messenger would be just that. In his fear, the man had been quick to put the blame on Thomas as the mastermind behind the forgery.

The gray dog trotted up and sat with a whine a little ways from Justice. He had smelled the meat and was eager to have a share. Smiling, Justice broke off a piece of the meat pie. Placing it in his palm, he crouched down, and the dog came forward grinning.

"Don't give that to him!" Gobi shouted, hurrying towards

them.

Justice closed his hand quickly. The dog, whining and dancing about, licked Justice's hand eagerly.

"He is hungry." Justice watched Gobi curiously.

"He can't eat that." Gobi tried to pull the dog away, but it squirmed from his arm and ran back to Justice.

"Why?" Justice rose and towered over the little man. It dawned on him that this was the only food he had been offered since coming to the town. The way it was given was suspicious, and it had come right after he had discovered the messenger. He looked at the meat pie; he had already eaten more than half of it.

"I think he will like it," Justice started to lower the bigger piece towards the dog.

"No!" Gobi protested sharply. He lowered his voice, still trying to pull the squirming dog away from Justice. "Please don't give it to him. I'm... well he's..." Gobi could not find the words.

"I will not give it to him if you tell me who killed Woodson, Dion, and Blair."

Gobi looked around. "It won't matter now if you know. Thomas killed them. And he will kill you if you don't leave. Can you not see that you are not wanted here?"

"Do you not see the death and pain caused by your choice to obey Thomas instead of the king?" Justice asked him seriously, as Gobi stooped and put his arms around the dog. With a grunt, he picked up the animal and staggered away.

Justice threw the meat pastry up onto a thatched roof where it would be out of the gray dog's reach and started walking. His strides long and purposeful, he could feel the poison at work. His stomach churned angrily and sweat broke out on his forehead. Passing Thomas' house without pausing, he charged into the underbrush beyond the graves. Following the narrow trail, he made his way to a little clearing he had discovered the night before. Unmindful of the boy sitting cross-legged in the leaves, Justice dropped to his knees and looked hard at the tangle of green before him. He had seen them there before. There! He grabbed a cluster of bright green berries.

"Those will make you throw up, don't..."

Justice had already shoved the berries into his mouth.

"Eat them," The boy finished dully.

Justice's face puckered as he ground the berries in his teeth.

The boy rose and moved away, watching in disgust as Justice cleared his stomach into the underbrush.

Having eaten more berries than necessary, it was several minutes before Justice could control the violent heaving of his stomach. Exhausted, he flopped to his back and closed his eyes.

"Must have been something pretty bad to make you go through all that to get it back out," the boy observed.

Until that moment, Justice had been unaware that he was not alone. He moved as if to get up, saw the boy, and flopped back down with a tired groan.

"Want some water?" Keeping his distance, the boy held out a hollowed gourd with a cork in its stem.

Justice did, but he was not willing to make the same mistake twice. Instead, he shook his head, no.

The boy chose a log upwind and sat watching the stranger.

"You talked to my mom last night," The boy observed, resuming his whittling.

Turning his head, Justice got a better look at the boy. He judged him to be around the age of ten. His hair was combed neatly to the side and though he appeared to be well cared for, Justice could see his face had been streaked with recent tears.

"You broke the twig to keep her from talking." Justice's voice was raspy.

The boy came over and knelt by him. Uncorking the gourd, he took a long drink. "See, it is not poison."

Justice raised himself on one elbow and took the water the boy held out.

"You can have it all," the boy said moving back to his log. "After what you just did, I'm going to wash it before I use it again."

Sitting up, Justice eyed him with amusement. Pouring a little of the water into his hand, Justice washed his mouth and chin. His stomach was unsettled, but the burning sensation had faded. The effects of the poison would be mild. "Why did you stop your mom from talking to me last night?"

Shrugging, the boy did not answer. He tested the two sticks he had been whittling to see how they fit. He was making a cross.

"What is your name?"

"Kyle," the boy answered, offering no family name.

"Kyle, will you tell me what happened?"

The boy looked at Justice with a wizened expression and nodded.

———

"We must find water soon. The canteen is almost empty." Martin informed Milo who had kept them at a driving pace all morning.

"You drink too much," Milo answered without stopping.

"There are four of us using this canteen," Martin answered. "We are not pack animals to be driven along."

Milo glared at him threateningly. "Do not cross me again."

Martin would have said more, but Sadie's hand on his arm stopped him.

Their band moved on wearily.

Kore walked alone, miserable and silent. He hated what was happening, but saw no way he could have avoided it. It was Milo and Rats who pushed themselves into their band. After all, he was protecting Anna Lea by allowing Milo to join them. He would have taken her days ago if Kore had not done as Milo had said.

He thought moodily about what Justice had said about becoming a subject of the king. Though he did not want to admit it, he could see a difference between those who had offered themselves as subjects and those who merely lived under the king's power. Anna Lea and the Becketts were subjects, while Milo and Rats ran their own lives, indifferent to the rules of the king. And he? Kore pushed the thought away. He would think about it later. He had enough on his mind already.

———

Justice ducked between the large stones that created his airy cave. The messenger had escaped, and all sign of the official letters and wax had been removed. If only Justice had brought another man to guard him. He thought again of the king's advice to travel in pairs. Why had Justice been so stubbornly against it? After hearing the story of the murder from Kyle, Justice had returned to retrieve the messenger he had left tied. When he found no sign of the man, Justice knew that Thomas was one step ahead of him. The poisoned food would have gotten Justice out of the way long enough for them to cover their tracks. Feeling in his pouch, Justice pulled out the king's seal. They would come for it. Expecting him to be weak and half dead, they would charge him. Once it was back in their hands, they would move closer to the outskirts to wield their traitorous power, bringing distrust and disgrace to the king's name.

Moving to the fire ring, Justice pulled one of the rocks from the circle on the floor. Using a sturdy stick, he dug out a crevice in the floor of his hideout that was several inches deep. He worked carefully beside the small fire so as to avoid scorching his hands. Removing his empty money pouch, Justice tucked the seal inside, glancing around to ensure no one was watching. Placing the pouch into the crevice he had made, He pushed the dirt back into place with the stick. Fresh dirt on his hands would give him away. Using his boot, he smoothed some of the lighter dirt over the place to cover the darker dirt he had upturned. Covering his work with the stone he had removed, Justice stepped on the stone, pressing it down and packing the earth beneath it. Using the same stick, Justice spread the burning wood of the fire so that it would heat the stones around it. Stepping back, he surveyed his work. It was enough.

Justice went to one of the many openings and looked down at the village sprawled out below. Kyle had told him that there had been great confusion when the villagers started receiving official letters from the king demanding that they pay the new tax or lose possession of their farms.

Afraid of the consequences of crossing the king, they had paid, borrowing money from Thomas to meet the required sum. Borrowing more than they could ever repay, and thus falling into a slave-like existence under his growing authority.

Woodson, Dion, and Blair were different. They knew the heart of the king and protested the sudden, heavy taxation. Having caught the messenger conferring with Thomas and expecting the other villagers to come forward for the truth, Woodson, Dion and Blair publically accused Thomas of using the messenger's authority for his own gain. No one stood with them. Many were already heavily indebted to Thomas and dared not speak against him. Their farms were their lives and livelihood.

In a rage, Thomas commanded the villagers to return to their houses. There was no one there to witness the death of the three men. But many had seen the animal like gleam in Thomas' eyes.

CHAPTER 16

"Brutus, I'm glad you could come." Thomas greeted, as the man bearing the king's emblem rode into town. "There has been terrible unrest in our little village since Justice, the King's Man, arrived. We have proof that he has been holding this man captive and forcing him to write false messages in the name of the king. He has demanded the villagers pay staggering sums and even sentenced to death an innocent man in order to cover up the untimely deaths of three of the king's subjects."

Frowning, Brutus reached down from his saddle and took the letters from the trembling messenger.

"I never would have done it," he sputtered pathetically. At first I thought he was acting on behalf of the king, after all, he bears the king's emblem, as do you. When I discovered he was a traitor, I tried to cross him. I had nothing to lose. What is my life compared to the reputation of the king? But Justice threatened the lives of the villagers and I did not know what to do. I could not allow them to be killed in my place. It was when he demanded a letter authorizing him to take the life of Martin Beckett, I knew I had to escape even if it cost me everything!"

Their meeting was in the open square, in full sight of the villagers who watched with interest. Had the inquisitive King's Man really been behind the plot all along?

"It is a serious accusation," Brutus frowned. "What evidence do you have to convict Justice?"

"It is he who carries the king's seal."

Several villagers murmured together at the shocking news.

"Where can I find him?" Brutus' eyes swept over the villagers.

Thomas pointed toward the mountain. "He has a camp at the top of the first ridge. The messenger has told me he is often summoned there to receive orders where Justice's plans will not be overheard."

Brutus nodded darkly, "The hour of reckoning has come."

———

Justice's horse nickered outside, drawing his attention from the village below. Someone was coming up the path. Justice tossed the stick he still held down into the brush below. Moving quickly, Justice patted his face briskly to give himself a flushed appearance. Flicking water from his canteen on to his forehead, he sat on his blanket and slouched against the boulder behind him. Gripping his stomach, he relaxed, slumping lower, and waited.

As the footsteps drew nearer, they also slowed.

Justice listened with his eyes half closed to the low conversation that was carried on outside. It was Brutus, sword drawn, who ducked through the low entrance first. His eyes expertly scanned the camp, coming to rest on the slumped form of his enemy. Beckoning the others inside, Brutus moved forward cautiously.

Brutus bumped Justice's boot with his own. Groaning, Justice made a weak attempt to open his eyes. He noticed that for the first time since they had met, Thomas was wearing a sword.

"Justice Spear," Brutus' deep voice carried authority he

did not represent. "You have been accused of stealing the king's seal and using its power for your own gain. How do you answer?"

Justice moaned and attempted to rise, falling back once more against the boulder that supported him.

"The poison has done its job," Thomas observed cruelly.

Brutus was not convinced. "Get the seal from his pouch. If it is on him as you say, it is all the evidence we need to carry out the king's judgment."

Thomas nudged the messenger who went hesitantly forward. Keeping an eye on Justice, he undid the clasp of the pouch and reached his hand inside and felt around. He turned to face them, his eyes wide with alarm. "It is not here."

"You said he had it." Thomas came forward, pushing the messenger aside. He plunged his hand into Justice's pouch and pulled out three letters. Two bore the broken seal of the king, the third was smeared with wax and had not been opened. Tossing the letters aside, he reached in once more. A coin sized pebble was all that remained.

"He must have hidden it somewhere." Thomas looked around the camp. Hurrying to the saddle, he emptied the meager contents of the saddle bags, feeling in all the crevices of the saddle, even those that were too small to conceal the metal seal. He rose, his eyes darting around in search of anything out of place. The fire crackled and hissed as if mocking him. "It must be here."

"You do not need the seal to kill him." Brutus' tone was chilling. He had lost nothing and did not pity the lean man who had sent for him. "We will say we found it, and have sent it back to the king by the messenger."

"But without the seal I am ruined," Thomas growled.

"You have enough money to live comfortably for some time," Brutus observed. "I understand that most of the farms belong to you already."

Thomas fumed. "But without the seal..." he was digging around the base of the rocks now, unwilling to give up his link to the king's power.

"What about me?" the messenger asked, suddenly recognizing the delicacy of his situation. He was the loose end, the only witness and accomplice to Thomas' crimes.

Brutus' look filled him with terror.

"No, you can't do it, I am the king's messenger. Send me away as you said. I will stick to your story. I swear, I won't come back."

Thomas looked at him with the same expression he had worn the night he killed Woodson, Dion, and Blair. "What story?" Thomas asked drawing his sword.

"No, Thomas, I made you rich. I did everything you said!" He turned and ran, stumbling in his haste. Thomas, followed him out, his steps swift and sure.

Brutus waited and soon heard a cry as the messenger met his deserved end.

Coldly turning back to the moaning King's Man at his feet, Brutus spoke the words that would allow him, by rule of the king, to kill his old enemy. "Justice Spear, you are under arrest for the traitorous misuse of the king's messenger and his royal seal. By the right of the king's law, I sentence you to death." He grinned and added, "To be carried out at once."

Grabbing Justice just below his jaw, Brutus pulled Justice to his feet.

Standing, but wavering unsteadily, Justice leaned weakly against the boulder and allowed his head to roll back against the stone.

"I have waited a long time for this, Justice." Brutus turned as Thomas ducked into the camp. The lean man's sword was bloodied.

Thomas met his cruel gaze. "I sent the seal back with him as you..." he stopped short, his eyes wide.

Brutus spun to face Justice. No longer lethargic and dying, Justice had moved away and stood ready to face them.

"Which one of you traitors prefers to die first?" Justice asked drawing his sword.

Brutus' low laugh echoed from the rocks that surrounded them. "Very clever Justice. You have won this time, but it will not be the last."

"What are you talking about?" Thomas demanded. "Kill him."

"The king's law does not allow me to kill him." Brutus' face mocked the law, even as he twisted it for his own use.

"Kill him!" Thomas ordered, shaking with rage.

"There is no proof of his crime." Brutus taunted, his eyes hard. He had learned long ago that when Justice drew his sword for the honor of the king, there was no one who could stand against him. "Once you are dead, the king's honor will be restored Thomas."

"Coward," Thomas spat, his eyes deadly. "I will deal with you shortly."

Brutus' face grew dark, "No one speaks against me and lives."

Justice's strong voice cut through the tense silence, drawing their attention back to where he stood. "Thomas Jacobs, today I have found evidence and witnesses enough to condemn you for your crimes. On your honor, did you kill Woodson, Dion, and Blair?"

Thomas glared hatefully at Justice, raising his bloodstained sword. "Yes I did, but my secret will die with you."

Justice, unfazed by the threat, went on. "Did you use the king's seal to divert justice and bring harm to his subjects?"

"I did, and I will use it again." Thomas taunted, his movements were calculated and deadly. "You will pay with your life. I will find that seal."

Justice, keeping an eye on Brutus who stood by the entrance, moved away from the rock wall to give himself more room to wield his blade. They circled, sizing up the battle to come.

"Thomas Jacobs, by your own admission you are guilty of murdering Woodson, Dion, and Blair..."

Brutus rolled his eyes. "Just kill him, Justice, you don't have to give him the speech."

"...and using the king's seal to dishonor his name and bring harm to his subjects." Justice kept his distance from Brutus as he dodged Thomas' thrust. The man was unpredictable and dangerous.

"By the authority of the king's law," Justice continued. The blades clashed together and they pressed against them, each testing the strength of his opponent.

They glared into each other's eyes as Justice spoke the final words. "I sentence you to death."

The words were scarcely out of his mouth before Justice pivoted sharply, causing Thomas to stumble to catch his balance. Barely managing to block the arching blow Justice brought down on him, Thomas righted himself, his dark eyes shining with hate. Again and again their blades met until the walls echoed with the sound.

"You bested me here by playing along with his story," Brutus informed Justice, gesturing with the tip of his sword to Thomas who brought his blade down heavily. Justice stumbled and retreated a few feet.

"Nice to hear you say it," Justice grunted as he took back the ground, driving Thomas back with rapid, well-placed blows that Thomas was forced to block.

"But you have not won," Brutus went on. "I have something of much more value that I have already taken from you."

"I have nothing of value for you to take," Justice responded, his breathing was heavier now. The battle had ranged all over the little camp. Both men were careful to stay out of range of Brutus' blade which waved lazily in the air. Thomas was tiring and Justice could feel it.

"Nothing? Poor Justice, you allowed yourself to care again, didn't you."

Justice made no answer. The fight was nearing its end and required his full focus. One mistake would cost him his life.

Thomas was skilled with the blade and fought desperately for his life, but he could not withstand the strength of Justice. The death blow was struck, and Thomas crumpled to the ground never to rise again.

Breathing hard, Justice moved unsteadily to lean against the wall. Though he would not admit it, the poison had not been without effect. The battle had been won, but he knew in his heart he did not have the strength for another.

"You will not fool me again," Brutus eyed him without mercy. "Poor Justice, you are tied down by your own goodness. You cannot leave this cave without the king's seal. You cannot leave the town without finding someone to right the wrongs. You cannot save the girl because you are too late." Brutus allowed the thought to sink in and breed fear in his opponent's mind. "Or were you not aware that there is a price on the head of that brainless simpleton?"

"Who would pay for her?" Justice asked incredulously, buying himself time to recover.

"A greater simpleton than she is," Brutus cringed, remembering her behavior at the inn. "We would make a good team, you and I. Will you not reconsider my offer? There are great riches and fame to be had if one is willing to deviate slightly from serving the king."

Justice drew himself up to his full height and faced Brutus boldly. "I belong to the king, Brutus, not by duty, but by choice. I will not serve another, even myself."

A sour look came over Brutus as if the words were distasteful. "Waste your life then." He spat, moving towards where Justice stood, "Serve your king and save his worthless villagers who will forget you tomorrow. I will build myself a fortune and a name that will endure long after I am gone."

Brutus leaped at him and Justice's sword sliced the air. Their blades met, an echoing clash. They stood, leaning against their crossed blades, their eyes locked.

"One day I will kill you," Brutus threatened darkly. He stepped back and Justice let him go.

Moving out of range, Brutus' tone became indifferent. "I would fight you now, Justice, but you would be fighting for your own dignity. The threat to the king's honor is no more. And, if I remember right," Brutus scoffed, "your honor is not worth defending."

Justice waited tensely for Brutus' next move.

"I am not greedy. You may have the meager coins in the village below. I have the girl, and am satisfied with the ransom she will bring." Without another word, he turned, ducked out of the cave, and strode off down the path.

Sheathing his sword, Justice quickly shoved the letters back into his pouch. Slinging his canteen strap over his shoulder, he retrieved the king's saddle. He did not have time to gather the things Thomas had removed from his saddle bags and had strewn about in his search. The heavy clop of the horse's hooves, reached his ears, and Justice whistled sharply. The sound stopped instantly.

"Leave the horse," Justice commanded loudly, not bothering to step outside.

Shifting the saddle to one arm, Justice drew his sword and listened. Hearing nothing, he ducked quickly through the opening, ready to face an ambush. His precautions were unnecessary. Brutus was moving quickly down the mountain to where his own horse was tied and waiting. Justice saddled his mount and checked Brutus' progress once more.

Slipping back into the cave, Justice pried up the stone

with the end of his sword. The little fire had died down, but the stones still held its heat. In moments, he held the little pouch containing the seal of the king. Fastening it to his belt, he paused to listen. Sensing no cause for alarm, the horse was cropping lazily at the underbrush. Slipping out of the cave, Justice mounted at once and hurried the horse down the mountain.

CHAPTER 17

"Thomas Jacobs is dead," Justice announced loudly. At his feet sat the heavy iron box he had retrieved from Thomas' house. It contained what was left of the money he had stolen from the people.

The square was almost empty. The few people who lingered there stared at him in disbelief. Justice saw in their faces a mixture of fear and relief.

"Gather the others, I do not have much time to settle the matter. I am needed at the Weaver's Refuge."

The crowd grew as children were sent throughout the village to spread the news. In minutes, most of the villagers were gathered in the square, talking and murmuring amongst themselves.

"Subjects of the king," Justice called loudly.

The noise died down, and they looked at him expectantly.

"Thomas Jacobs has paid the price set by the king for murder. I understand that Thomas and the disloyal messenger used the king's seal to cheat you out of your farms and lands."

Still the people stared and said nothing.

"I cannot stay to sort out how much each has lost. You must vote together on three men who can be trusted to handle the task."

Hope lit the eyes of the villagers and they glanced at one another in surprise. They had been under Thomas' rule for so long that having a choice seemed like a luxury.

"I say Earl. Anyone agree?" A farmer, still holding his shovel, pushed the man beside him forward.

"Yes, Earl can be trusted!" Several others chimed in.

"Raise your hand if you are satisfied with Earl being the first of the three," Justice instructed.

Hands went up all over the square.

"Raise your hand if you have an objection."

A small child raised her hand, her face bright with excitement. A laugh rippled through the villagers as her blushing mother pushed the little hand down again.

"Who else?" Justice knew Brutus was already galloping along the King's Highway.

"How about Brook? She's not a man but she knows her money."

The others agreed as one.

"Quickly, one more," Justice urged, handing the key to the box to the first man chosen.

There was a few moments of discussion before the last man was chosen.

"You three are elected as treasurers of this village." Justice mounted and rode over to the man with the shovel. "There are two bodies on the mountain. Will you see that they are buried?"

The man nodded seriously.

"For the king and his honor!" Justice shouted, urging his horse forward. The villagers parted, applauding him as a hero as he galloped off towards the King's Highway.

———

"Turn here," Milo instructed pointing to a road that veered off from the King's Highway.

The little band stopped and blinked at him in surprise.

"The Weaver's Refuge is…" Kore dropped his hand to his side. No one had bothered to look where he had pointed.

"Is this way," Milo indicated the side road once more.

"Justice said nothing about leaving the King's Highway," Martin pointed out firmly.

"Did he not say three days journey on the King's Highway?" Milo's tone was too pleasant.

"He did."

"This is the third day, and here is the path to the Refuge."

As they spoke, Kore worked his way to Martin's side. The hunting knife was the only weapon they had between them.

"We will not leave the highway," Martin informed him.

"Not even for an inn with a warm bath and good food?" Milo laughed. "You are too serious, Martin. We could all use the refreshment."

A traveler pulling a hand cart excused himself as he passed. He was heading on up the King's Highway where Martin insisted they go.

"Sir, is that the way to the Weaver's Refuge?"

"It is." The traveler did not stop. "The sign has been removed, but the king's soldiers will replace it."

Martin looked at Milo, his expression one of anger and distrust. "We will go on to the Weaver's Refuge. There will be refreshment there."

Milo's silky pleasantries vanished. He struck Martin, knocking him to the ground. Martin scrambled to his feet and grabbed for his hunting knife, it was gone. His eyes darted to Kore and then to the knife in the young man's hand.

Milo struck him again, sending Martin stumbling into the ditch beside the road. He turned to grab Anna Lea but found Kore standing between them.

"That's enough," Kore's voice wavered, but his face was determined.

Milo turned on him, his huge form making Kore look

small and childlike before him. "Get out of my way, boy."

Kore held the knife unsteadily, trembling before Milo's hateful look. "We are going to the Weaver's Refuge. That is what we agreed upon. You will get your reward there. You can have my share."

Martin, moving around behind Milo, stood ready, waiting for his chance.

"That is where we are going, Kore," Milo informed him, his voice softening. "We will stop here for the night and continue on in the morning."

"You are lying." Kore braced himself and glared up at Milo. "Anna Lea is with me. Justice told me to take her to the Weaver's Refuge, and that is what I will do."

Milo laughed, "Justice, eh? And where is he? Left you to do his dirty work and play nursemaid to the ladies while he trotted off to do a man's work."

Kore wavered, and Milo saw it.

"Justice is using you, Kore. Tricking you with lies about the king and his subjects. The king's reward will be nothing compared to the ransom Brutus has arranged."

"It's not true, Kore," Martin dodged the big man's backhand that would have sent him sprawling once more. "The king's ways work. They bring peace and happiness. You must stand for truth, Kore. Trust Justice. He would not lie to you." He dodged again, stumbling and catching himself with his hand. Milo lunged at Martin and struck him hard. Martin faltered on the edge of the steep ditch, trying desperately to regain his balance. Milo shoved him hard. Crying out as he fell, Martin's head struck a rock hidden in the long grass, and he lay still.

"Martin!" Sadie rushed down to him, stumbling in her haste.

"Is he okay?" Kore called when she reached the place where Martin lay.

"He is breathing." They heard the relief in her voice.

"Forget about them, Kore." Milo tried to move around him to reach Anna Lea, but Kore pivoted with him. "You want the reward, don't you? Or do you prefer this life of eating roots along the King's Highway that Justice has offered."

"Justice is a good man," Kore moved again to keep himself between Milo and Anna Lea.

"He killed your father, didn't he?" Milo locked eyes with Kore. "What will keep him from killing you?"

Kore looked away, shaking his head. He could not think about this now.

Milo saw his chance and lunged. Grabbing Kore's arm, he twisted it until the knife dropped to the ground. Shoving Kore away, Milo retrieved the knife. "You had better choose whose side you are on."

Holding his sore arm, Kore bit his lip angrily. Milo was right. If Justice had not left them alone, they would not be in this trouble.

"I don't have to trust anyone," Kore answered hotly. "I'm taking Anna Lea to the Weaver's Refuge. I'll do it alone if I have to." He grabbed her wrist and stormed off down the road pulling her along.

Milo laughed, "Admit it Kore. You are not a subject of the king. You are one of us."

Rats emerged from the bushes along the highway and moved to stand in their way. "That is not the right way, Kore." He held a pointed dagger which he thrust at them in little sharp jabs.

Kore had no choice but to back away from the sharp tip of the dagger. "I'm sorry, Anna Lea. I never meant for this to happen. They said we would get the reward at the Weaver's Refuge. I thought that you would be safe there." He glanced at her. She was pale, her eyes wide with fear.

"Don't let them take me, Kore. Please don't let them take

me." Her voice was almost inaudible.

Kore let go of her hand and dove at Rats, driving him to the ground. They wrestled for the blade, rolling in the dust together.

Anna Lea ran. She dodged past them, screaming desperately as Milo's big hand closed on the skirt of her dress. He jerked her back and grabbed her by the arm. "We just want to stop for the night, you don't mind that, do you?"

Though she struggled, she could not free herself from his strong grasp. Annoyed, Milo wrapped one arm around her slender waist and lifted her from the ground, holding her back tightly against his side where she could kick and struggle, but could not escape.

"It is hard to show hospitality sometimes," Milo told Rats who got up grinning and panting, knife in hand.

Anna Lea caught sight of Kore. He lay bleeding on the King's Highway. "You can't leave him!" She writhed frantically in the big man's arm.

"What do you want to help him for? He was in on the plan the whole time."

"He will die," Anna Lea sobbed.

"It serves him right for trying to cross me." Milo cocked his head at Rats who followed, wiping his dagger clean on the skirt of Anna Lea's dress.

CHAPTER 18

Justice rode hard. His horse, covered in lather, thundered down the King's Highway. He had traveled for almost two days, resting only briefly in the darkest hours of the night. Justice knew his mount could not keep up the breakneck pace for much longer. By horseback, the journey was only two days, and Justice could not afford to lose the horse now that he was so close.

Ahead of him, he saw a movement by the road and stood in his stirrups to get a better look. It was Brutus' horse, winded and lame, hobbling along through the tall grass. Its breath came in great wheezing gasps. As they passed, Justice looked back at the pitiful animal. He could do nothing for it now.

Justice sat back a little and his mount responded by slowing its pace. Justice pulled the animal to a stop and slid from the saddle. Walking by its head, he scanned the road for any sign of the little band he had sent ahead. Fresh wagon tracks had pressed a trail through the dry dust of the road. By the marks left by the hooves of the team pulling the wagon, Justice knew they had traveled very quickly. Brutus would be with them, urging them on with a handsome bribe. It was true that the life of a traitor seemed to be the life of ease. Brutus had all the money he needed and was not constrained by the rules of another.

Justice tried to pull the horse into a trot, but it refused, plodding steadily on. The animal's heavy breathing slowly subsided to a normal rhythm. The little band should have reached the Weaver's Refuge by now, even if they had stopped often along the way. Justice told himself. Perhaps Brutus had been bluffing about having Anna Lea. Inside, Justice knew it was he himself who was bluffing. Brutus was a cruel man, but he was also shrewd. He often employed others to get what he wanted.

Justice could not afford to allow himself to think on what Brutus could do. Fear stirred up by worry would cripple him before the battle had begun.

"Oh, King," Justice spoke the words softly, "I cannot reach them in time. They will need your protection."

As he walked, the horse's heavy breathing slowly subsided to a normal rhythm. To take his mind off of Brutus, Justice considered the benefits of traveling as a pair. Two King's Men would be much harder to conquer than one. Two would mean more money for food, and more..."

A sound broke through his thoughts. Looking back, he saw a cloud of dust that was quickly drawing nearer. Justice guided his horse to the side of the road. In the center of the cloud were two soldiers who pulled their mounts up sharply, kicking up a cloud of dust that drifted away on the wind. A third horse danced nervously on its lead behind them.

The soldier displayed the king's emblem on the collar of his uniform and then asked, "Are you Justice?" The soldier's brisk tone was hard to read.

"I am."

The soldier dismounted and took the lead of the prancing horse from his companion. "News of your work has reached the king. He has sent you this fresh mount to help you on your way. My companion will take your horse and follow at a pace it can bear. If you will permit me, I will travel with you and aid you as I can."

Justice blinked at them in surprise. How had the king

known? Why question the provision, Justice reminded himself. He is the king. Taking the reins of the fresh horse, Justice swung into the saddle.

"The canteen is full if you have need of it," the soldier offered, spurring his mount forward. Justice urged his horse to follow. It was fresh and eager and surged forward at the slightest prompting. They set the pace at a swift canter, riding side by side. Justice took a swig from the canteen and spit the dusty water from his mouth before taking a long drink of the cool water.

The soldier glanced at him but said nothing.

"How did you know I was here?" Justice replaced the lid of the canteen and secured it to the saddle.

"A strange, wide man who called himself Gobi, turned himself in at the guard post last night. He feared you had been killed." The soldier's eyes left the road briefly. "He said he came because of your mercy. Something about Gray and a pastry. He was agitated and his story was not very clear. The villagers told us what had happened, and that you were headed for the Weaver's Refuge."

"Thank you for coming." Looking over, Justice took in the features of his new companion. The man was taller than Justice. His thick black hair was short and neat. The man turned, and Justice quickly looked away. He did not miss the soldier's amused smile.

"The name is Gavin."

"I assume you have heard about Brutus?" Justice scanned the empty road ahead. The wagon tracks stretched ahead, still clear in the dust.

"The villager's thought you were pursuing him, but knew very little. Tell me what you know." Gavin prompted.

"Only that Brutus, who is no longer loyal to the king, believes kidnapping Anna Lea will somehow make him rich. Is that true?"

"It is true," Gavin confirmed sadly. "She is in great danger. The king has sent soldiers across the realm to bring her safely home."

Justice took another swig of water, giving himself time to process the information.

"You have traveled hard the last few days." Gavin observed with respect, "We have changed mounts three times in order to catch up to you. Reaching back, he unclasped his saddle bag and pulled something from inside.

Justice knew at once it was food.

"I thought you might need something to eat." Unwrapping the bread, Gavin looked over at Justice.

Justice searched the soldier's eyes. Was he a truly a loyal subject? Could it all be an elaborate set up by Brutus?

Gavin watched Justice as he wrestled inwardly with the decision. He had seen the trust disappear from the eyes of the King's Man who rode beside him. Breaking a piece off of the bread, Gavin held it up where Justice could see it well. "If it is poisoned, we will both die. If I live, it is safe." Gavin popped the piece of bread into his mouth before handing the thin loaf to Justice. Turning his attention back to the road, Gavin rode in silence, chewing contentedly.

Justice broke off a little piece and put it into his mouth. As if aroused by the taste, hunger gripped him. He felt light headed and gripped the saddle to steady himself.

"Hmm. You might need something a bit more substantial." Gavin twisted to retrieve something else from his saddle bag. Unwrapping it, he handed Justice a small piece of dried meat. "While you eat, I will tell you what I know."

Nodding, Justice accepted the meat without question.

"Anna Lea, as you called her, is actually Annalise Leona Hillcrest, daughter of the late Counselor and Lady Hillcrest."

Justice, taking another bite, waited for Gavin to go on.

"All of the lands and goods of the expansive Hillcrest

estate pass on to Annalise as the sole heir. Which makes her extremely wealthy," Gavin pointed out, in case Justice, distracted by the food, had missed the meaning. "Because there has been no news of Annalise since she disappeared the same night her parents were killed, many believed that she too had been killed. Now, over three years after her parents were murdered, someone has come forward claiming to have seen her alive. A reward has been offered for her safe return or any information leading the king's soldiers to her."

"And Brutus believes he can get the king to pay an even higher ransom for her life," Justice finished.

"That is what we fear," Gavin agreed.

They rode in silence, both considering the problem they would soon face.

Once he had eaten, Justice took another long drink from the canteen. He sighed heavily. It felt good to be full.

"The Weaver's Refuge is not far now," Gavin pointed ahead. He scanned the road with a frown. "The signpost has been removed."

Justice spotted the smaller road that veered to the left from the highway. Dismounting, he examined a dark stain in the dirt. It was at least a day old. He wondered who had been wounded. Brutus was right, Justice had allowed himself to care for the little band of travelers. "Ride ahead and confirm that they are not at the Weaver's Refuge," Justice instructed. "If they are not, this is the road they would have taken."

"How can you be sure?" Gavin asked, peering down the side road.

"There is blood there in the dust. Some band must have had a violent disagreement about which path they would take. Ride quickly and bring me word. I will check the inn to see if they are there."

With a salute, Gavin kicked his mount and galloped off down the road.

Justice, riding at a much slower pace so as not to raise suspicion, traveled down the side road marked with signs of an inn.

The yard was quiet as Justice entered. Pulling the weary horse to a stop, he looked around. The loaded wagon just beyond the inn caught his eye. Sliding from the saddle, Justice looped the reign around the fence post where the horse could reach fresh grass.

He went to the wagon. The fresh layer of dust confirmed his suspicions. Skirting the large inn, Justice let himself in through the back door. The cook shouted angrily as Justice slipped through the kitchen to the short hall that led to the dining room.

Standing in doorway he looked over the busy room. It was the supper hour, and the inn was bustling with travelers. Milo and Rats sat by themselves not far from the doorway where Justice stood. He drew back slightly and touched the hilt of his sword. The last time he had seen Milo was at his own burial. Steadied by its steely presence, Justice scanned the room once more, keeping the door frame between himself and Rats. The thin man's nervous eyes checked the doorway every few seconds. He was clearly expecting someone.

———

Anna Lea lay with her face to the wall. Across the room, Brutus and a pale man with spectacles were arguing together about the amount and terms of the ransom Brutus would demand. Over the single window was a lattice which cast a lacy pattern on the wall by her head. As they argued, Anna Lea lay unmoving, watching the patterned shadow as it crept slowly across the wall.

She could not close her eyes, for when she did, she would

see again the wounded Kore, lying bleeding on the road. A new sound drew her attention but not her eyes to the other side of the room. She heard the chairs scrape back from the narrow table. The men, talking in hushed tones now, agreed at last on the next steps of the plan. She heard them pause and knew without moving that they were looking at her. Another hushed conference was followed by the heavy tread of their feet as they left the room.

Anna Lea waited, listening intently. Two sets of boots descended the wooden staircase. One walked with a careless clumsy step while the other, belonging to Brutus, was purposeful and firm.

Springing from the bed, Anna Lea looked frantically around the room. She went to the window and inspected the possibility of escaping through the lattice. The room was on the second floor and there was nothing to break her fall except the hard ground below. Crossing the room once more, she peeked out the door. The hall was empty. Anna Lea slipped silently into the hall. She froze at the top of the stair. Brutus stood on the landing below her, giving the pale messenger some final details. This was her only chance of escape He would not leave her alone again. But where could she go?

CHAPTER 19

Justice looked out over the room, once more, keeping an eye on Rats. Milo sat with his back to the door. His plate was pushed back and his big feet were propped up lazily on the chair beside Rats.

Justice moved back into the hallway. There was no sign of Martin or Kore among the men who filled the room. Above him, Justice heard the unmistakable voice of Brutus. He was talking to someone on the landing over where Justice stood. Turning, Justice tried to catch sight of Brutus without giving himself away. Moving to get a better look, he bumped into a waiter coming from the kitchen.

"Justice!" the man exclaimed softly in amazement.

Looking at the waiter for the first time, Justice found himself looking at Martin Beckett.

"You are safe then!" Justice kept his voice low.

"Yes, but Kore was hurt badly." Martin matched his volume still holding the tray containing two pastries on plates. "He is at the Weaver's Refuge. We came for Anna Lea."

"We?"

A young man, wearing an apron and a scowl, rounded the corner, bumping into Martin and almost toppling his tray.

"Now look what you have done," Martin scolded. "Take these pastries out and don't drop them."

The unhappy youth took the tray Martin had been holding and opened his mouth to speak.

Cutting him off, Martin pointed toward the dining room. "Take them to the first table. And be quick about it."

"The table with that big man and the thin twitchy one?" the young man's scowl deepened.

"Watch how you talk about the customers, boy. Now hurry, or you will get the boxing you deserve from Cook."

"I'm taking it," he grumbled.

"Cook's special, on the house," Martin instructed.

Nodding to show he had heard, and muttering complaints, the boy trudged back toward the crowded room.

"That should make things a little easier." Without showing himself, Martin watched the boy to insure he got the table right.

Grabbing Martin's arm to pull his attention away from the food, Justice hissed, "Martin, where is Anna Lea?"

Martin pointed to the stairs above them.

———

Anna Lea backed away from the stairs to where she could not be seen by Brutus and his messenger. They had been looking down at the map the pale man held and had not seen her. Reaching for the closest doorknob, she hesitated. What if it were Milo or Rats' room? Fear gripped her. She could not take a chance like that, not now. She could tell the conversation below was almost over. Brutus would be coming back up the stairs. If only she had a weapon of some kind. Moving as quickly and as quietly as she could, Anna Lea moved to the far end of the hall. There was a window there. Perhaps there would be a tree or something she could climb onto.

The last door opened as she passed and a hand reached out for her arm. Anna Lea jerked away with a little cry.

Stumbling in her haste to get away.

"Anna Lea, Anna Lea," a familiar voice called softly, breaking through her panicked flight. "There is no time. Come quickly."

Anna Lea spun to see Sadie standing in the open doorway of the last room. "Hurry!" Sadie begged, beckoning her inside with a furtive glance at the stairs.

Anna Lea ran past her into the room and stood trembling by the window.

Shutting the door, Sadie propped a chair under the doorknob before turning to face Anna Lea. Though they were not far apart in age, Sadie looked at Anna Lea's frightened face with all the pity and love of a mother. Anna Lea sobbed once as Sadie hugged her tightly.

"Martin is here too," Sadie whispered without letting her go. "We came to help you."

"And Kore?" Anna Lea stepped back to look into Sadie's eyes.

"Kore was hurt badly, but he is safe now at the Weaver's Refuge."

In the hall Brutus bellowed angrily for Milo.

Anna Lea and Sadie froze, their faces filled with terror.

———

Drawing his sword, Justice stood ready, watching the stairs. He had no intention of being sandwiched between Milo and Brutus between the narrow banisters. A pale messenger, intent on his mission, had slipped past them moments before. By Brutus' tone, Justice could tell that his prize, the heir of Hillcrest estate, had escaped while he was absent. Though Anna Lea was convincing as a simpleton, by her cleverness, she had escaped from the great Brutus' himself.

Milo and Rats were slow in coming, and Brutus bellowed for them again. The dining room cleared quickly. Many had encountered Brutus' wrath before and wanted no part in it now. The doors above were being opened and slammed closed again.

"Go now! Milo and Rats are eating their pastries." Martin's tone caused Justice to look at him questioningly, but he offered no further information.

Taking the stairs two at a time, Justice paused on the landing until he heard another door open. Moving quickly, he emerged onto the empty hall. A moment later, Brutus came out of the room he had been searching. He stopped with his hand on the door when he caught sight of Justice.

"You." The single word was laced with hate. "You will not take this from me." Brutus drew his sword and faced Justice boldly.

Justice moved forward slowly, "Where is the girl?" he asked calmly.

Brutus just sneered at him.

"Give her to me," Justice instructed, still narrowing the gap between them.

"First my ransom," Brutus demanded.

Justice met his eyes without emotion, "Your life shall be your ransom."

"Not good enough, Justice." Brutus surged forward and their blades met. Their strength was well matched as they ranged up and down the narrow hall.

Justice drew back to block Brutus' attack. His arm struck the doorframe and the tip of Brutus' sword sunk painfully into his hip.

Flinching, Justice threw open the door and swung out of range. Their swords left gashes in the walls and bedframes as they battled for their lives. Again and again their swords met, each deadly blow parried at the last possible second.

Justice sprang forward, pushing his opponent back. Brutus' foot caught on the blanket that hung from the bed, and he fell hard. Scrambling to his feet, Brutus kept his blade between himself and Justice.

Seeing his chance, Justice hurled the chair through the lattice covering the window and dove through the opening. Rolling smoothly to his feet, on the low slanted roof, he faced the window, sword ready. Here he would have the space needed to manage his blade.

The second chair came crashing out causing Justice to jump out of the way. Brutus sprung through the opening. In one continuous motion, Brutus brought his blade down hard. Justice deflected the blow, but the force of it knocked him to one knee.

Jabbing at Brutus, Justice bought himself time to rise. The wound in his hip was not serious, but painful enough to hamper his movements. As they ranged across the rooftop, a crowd of the onlookers gathered below. Brutus shouted in rage as Justice's blade cut into his left side. He rushed forward, striking hard, pushing Justice closer and closer to the edge of the roof. When there was only a step left. Justice sprung backwards. The tip of Brutus' blade reached out after him. Twisting to avoid the cold steel, Justice landed hard. He was up in an instant. Bracing himself, Justice looked up at Brutus, silently challenging him to continue the fight.

Brutus did not follow. He knew his own strength was waning and dared not face Justice now.

Pacing like an angry lion on the edge of the roof, Brutus glared down at Justice. Beyond Justice, the king's soldiers stood ready, awaiting Justice's command.

"Have you had enough, Brutus?" Justice called up to him. He had spotted Anna Lea and Sadie standing with Martin a safe distance away. From the ground he could see the missing window lattice and the rope the ladies, had used to make their escape. "I have what I came for." Justice pointed his sword tip toward the ladies drawing Brutus' attention to them. "Because she is unharmed, the ransom is yours for the taking."

Brutus' jaw clenched in anger. He knew the ransom Justice spoke of was his own life.

"Throw down your ring, Brutus," Justice instructed. "Unless you are willing to go to the king and beg his pardon, you are no longer worthy to wear the king's emblem."

"I have chosen my path," Brutus growled darkly. Pulling the ring from his finger, he tossed it aside in haughty disdain.

Gavin came forward, and Justice momentarily took his eye from his pacing opponent on the rooftop. When they looked up again, Brutus was gone.

The second soldier Justice had met on the road came into view, riding slowly up the shaded lane. Beside him, head down, walked Justice's horse. The sweat had dried on the animal, leaving white patterns on the horse's dark coat. Justice whistled softly. The horse's ears flicked forward and it lifted its head, tugging at the lead held by the soldier. He looked at Justice for instructions. At a nod from the King's Man, the soldier slipped the lead rope from the horse's bridle.

The horse moved to Justice's side and stood ready.

"You are a faithful animal," Justice rested his hand for a moment on the horse's neck. Placing his foot in the stirrup, Justice pulled himself up into the saddle.

From where she stood, Anna Lea saw him wince as he mounted. "He is hurt," she whispered to Martin.

He nodded. "It is time for us to return to the Weavers Refuge," Martin announced, putting his arm around Sadie's waist. "Kore will be anxious to hear that Anna Lea is safe."

Justice looked at the little band, his band, and smiled. "You have done well." Gently urging his mount forward, Justice rode to where Gavin was speaking to a knot of soldiers.

Gavin turned to him expectantly.

"What of Milo and Rats?"

"My men have arrested them both. It seems the rich food was too much for them after their long journey. Both were asleep at the table."

Justice looked back at Martin and caught him grinning mischievously.

"Have a man retrieve Brutus' ring from the rooftop. It belongs once more to the king."

Gavin communicated the order, and two soldiers hurried to obey.

"Thank you, Gavin. It was an honor to ride beside you. I could not have done it without your help."

A broad smile spread across the soldier's face. "I look forward to working with you in the future." Gavin extended his hand, and Justice leaned down to shake it. "We are the king's subjects, and we stand for the king's honor. As long as we are working for him, we are working together."

Justice nodded with a smile. Walking his mount back to the band awaiting him, Justice turned to face the soldiers once more. His strong voice carried well in the quiet evening, "For the king's honor!"

They joined heartily in the response, "For the honor of the king!"

CHAPTER 20

"And here he is, getting along quite well today." The plump lady pushed open the door and stood holding it open. Her hair was pulled up into a knot and held in place by a narrow, silver pin. She smiled and nodded at Kore, then turned and left them alone.

"Justice!" Kore exclaimed happily. He saw the crutch and frowned. "What happened to you?"

Justice, moving awkwardly with the help of a single crutch, made his way to the wooden chair beside Kore's bed.

"Oh, nothing serious. I wanted a little of the sympathy I heard you were getting here," Justice answered with a laugh.

"He jumped off a roof," Martin said from the doorway. "Mind if I join you?"

Eyes shining, Kore looked across at him. "Please do! I thought…" he lowered his gaze for a moment. "I did not know if you had made it. When you were down in that ditch."

"Yes, and I came up to find you all sliced up like a loaf of bread," Martin responded, leaning against the wall by the door.

"There are only two cuts on my chest," Kore corrected. "I'm sorry for all the trouble I caused, Martin. I should have told you what was going on."

"You have learned an important lesson, Kore. We will leave it at that, knowing you will not make the same mistake in the future."

Kore nodded gratefully, turning his head to face Justice.

"If I make it through, will you teach me to handle a blade?"

Justice grinned at Kore's eagerness. He was glad to see the injuries had not dampened his spirit. "Get well, and we will talk about it again."

"What about you, Justice? Why did you jump off a roof?" Kore asked. They could see he was tiring.

"You should have seen it," Martin cut in before Justice could respond. "Justice and Brutus fought all through the inn, slicing and stabbing walls everywhere!"

Kore glanced at Justice. The eyes of the once stoic King's Man shone with silent laughter. Looking over at Kore, he shook his head with a grin.

"Eventually the fight moved out on the roof and Brutus was swinging hard, pushing Justice toward the edge." Lost in his story, Martin sprang forward, swinging an invisible sword in short, driving strokes. "Justice had no room, he was teetering on the edge of the roof..." Martin teetered, looking desperately over his shoulder as if he were about to fall.

A movement at the door drew his attention, and Martin stopped his teetering act to welcome Sadie and Anna Lea who stood uncertainly in the doorway. They looked clean and refreshed. Anna Lea's hair was pulled back as it had been when Justice first saw her with its waves falling to her shoulders. Her simple green gown fit her well. She was the heir of an estate now, a lady. Sadie, standing beside her, grinned at Martin playfully. "And then what happened? Did he fall from the rooftop?"

Martin's eyes were laughing as he continued his animated tale. "Then he jumped!" Martin had self-consciously stopped his charade when the ladies arrived. "He rolled to his feet and stood challenging Brutus who was still on the roof. Only one knew that in landing the leap, Justice had badly sprained his ankle." Martin looked at Justice in admiration. "He never let on. Brutus believed he was beaten, and retreated while he still could."

Kore lay pale and quiet, but his eyes followed Martin through the telling. "What of Milo and Rats?" His voice was weak now.

"Martin drugged them with pastries from the kitchen." It was Justice's turn to tell. "They were asleep at the table when the soldiers came for them. They will be sentenced by the king at his judgment seat."

The plump woman returned. She went to the bed, looking concerned.

"You must come again another time. His wounds are serious, but with rest and care he will soon recover." She ushered them out, adding in a confidential tone, "Many are brought here wounded and alone. Their recovery is slow and painful. Those who have someone to care about heal much faster." She looked around at them and laughed gently. "Kore will heal quickly with a jolly band like this at his side."

Justice remembered the words of Gavin, "We are the king's subjects, and we stand for the king's honor. As long as we are working for him, we are working together."

Justice looked in at Kore from the hall and said softly. "For the king's honor."

Kore's eyes fluttered open, and he smiled weakly at Justice. Taking a painful breath, he whispered back, "For the honor of the king!"

———

Brutus stood glowering at the King's Highway. No matter how close the battle, Justice always came out on top. And the insult of Justice demanding his ring. Brutus rubbed his empty finger and spat contemptuously on the dusty road. He had not meant to give it to Justice. In his anger, he had wrenched it off and hurled it away without thinking.

It had not belonged to him. Brutus' frown darkened. He had worn it for himself and not the king from the start. The vow to the king had been a show. It was expected. Everyone said he would follow in the footsteps of his father who had died in the service of the king. A sly smile slid into place and Brutus rubbed his beard. He had knelt beside Justice and sworn allegiance to a king he had no intention of serving. It had all been a lie. Brutus knew the power of a King's Man. He knew the respect the ring and sword brought to their owner.

A movement up the road caught Brutus' attention. A lone traveler was approaching. The little cloud of dust gave him away long before Brutus could make out the form of a man. Brutus' hand went to the hilt of his sword. A traveler would mean money. It would be easy pickings. It was illegal to rob someone on the King's Highway, but Brutus still had the sword of the king and knew he would face very little resistance. The sword hilt was cold to the touch, and Brutus cringed. This too was a lie. He had used the kings' name, and the king's emblem. Brutus had built himself a name. He had built himself a reputation that was feared by most. All the while knowing that what he did was fake and empty.

Brutus waited, watching the traveler. As the man approached, something inside of Brutus thrilled with expectation, while at the same time he cringed. Even from a distance, Brutus knew it was the king himself. The king was not wearing costly garments or even his crown. Instead, he was dressed in the common dull clothes of a commoner.

Brutus stood undecided. He knew the king would not be pleased. He had not seen the king in years. The king's network was strong, and surely Brutus' acts of treachery had reached the king long ago.

Before he could decide what to do, the king had approached him. He stopped and looked at Brutus. Braced for disapproval, Brutus was not prepared for the intense love in the king's eyes. How could he have betrayed such a king? A longing welled up inside him that surprised Brutus. He wanted desperately to serve the king. He was tired of forcing people to fear him. Tired of living a lie as a King's Man. After all the years of mocking the king, Brutus was cut to the heart by the king's kind eyes.

It was the king who spoke first. "You lost your ring, Brutus." He paused and added gently, "and you were considering losing me."

Brutus shifted uncomfortably, overwhelmed by the king's powerful look of love. There was no condemnation, only love, tainted slightly by a hint of sadness. The king was right. Brutus stood at the mouth of the road leading from the King's Highway to the outskirts. There, those who chose to turn from the king lived in rebellion. Those who took this path, never returned to the king's realm again.

"Long ago, you spoke words before me that you did not mean."

Out of habit, Brutus opened his mouth to defend himself.

The king shook his head, "Of course I knew, Brutus. There are many who act as if they belong to me. There is no power in a life of deceit. You must become my subject before you can truly serve me. Brutus, you have lived under your own rules and found that life does not satisfy. That is why I have come. I came to invite you to serve me. To truly serve me." He stood tall and powerful before Brutus. Even in the clothes of a common villager, there was no mistaking the authority he held. "You have no power to come to me on your own, Brutus. I gave you that longing for my service when you were a child. You have resisted it for many years. Now, you are here at the crossroads, and I am offering you life. A hard, adventurous life full of people who hate you for my sake."

Brutus smiled a little, "I would have chosen a more appealing description if I wanted to convince someone to join me."

The king smiled, and it seemed the sun shone a little brighter above them. "I will not lie to you, Brutus. The life of a King's Man is not an easy life. You have seen what it can cost. But know this. Through it all, no matter what you face, my power will strengthen and back you when you walk in my way."

Something in Brutus awakened. There on the King's Highway, where a few minutes before he had been deciding whether or not to step into the land of the outskirts and leave the king forever, everything became clear. No matter what Brutus did, he could not defeat Justice. He saw now that it was not Justice he was fighting against. It was the power of the king himself.

The loving eyes of the king melted the hard shell of a life Brutus had created for himself. He had tasted the life of self and found that beneath the outer glow, it was shallow and bitter. He wanted no more of it. For a moment, they stood facing one another without speaking. And then, slowly, Brutus dropped to one knee before the king. There would be no more pretending.

CHAPTER 21

"Kore? May I come in?"

There was a moment of hesitation before a woman's voice called softly, "Come in."

Anna Lea pushed open the door. There, by Kore's bed was a beautiful woman. The simple dress she wore could not hide the nobility of the lady.

Anna Lea's eyes moved from Kore's face on the pillow to the beautiful face of the stranger. Their features were similar. "You are Kore's mother."

She smiled, "I am. And you must be Annalise. Kore has spoken very highly of you."

Anna Lea glanced at Kore. His face reddened slightly, but he did not look up. He had not met her eyes since she entered the room. Was he ashamed that she should meet his mother? Several weeks had passed since they had arrived at the Weaver's Refuge. In all that time, Anna Lea had never seen Kore's mother.

"It will take me some time to get used to my old name," Anna Lea giggled and was rewarded by a startled look of panic from Kore.

Grinning mischievously at him, Anna Lea refrained from snorting. "I thought maybe you did not hear me come in," she explained, her eyes laughing.

"Yes, I heard you." He was annoyed to have fallen for her trick. "You might as well sit down."

Anna Lea took the open chair, watching him expectantly.

Kore let his breath out slowly. "Anna Lea, this is my mother, Lady Dahliah Eston."

"Not a lady anymore," Dahliah corrected gently with a hand on Kore's arm. She looked over at Anna Lea. "I gave up the title and came here when Kore's father was killed. I am sure Kore has told you."

"No, he did not. Kore spoke very little of his family."

"And you spoke very little of yours," Kore pointed out bluntly.

"Kore that is no way to speak to a lady," Dahliah corrected. "Kore and I moved here to the outskirts because I feared what happened to his father would happen to him."

A light knock on the door drew their attention.

Dahlia's hand flew to her mouth and rose with a little cry.

"I did not mean to startle you, Lady Eston." Justice had stepped back, as if to lessen the pain his presence awoke. "I did not come to bring harm." He hesitated, as if unsure, and then turned to go.

"Justice, wait," Anna Lea called after him. He paused with his back to them.

"Can he not come in Lady Eston? He and I are leaving for the palace soon. His ankle has healed enough to travel. Justice did not mean to scare you. He only wanted to say goodbye to Kore. That is what I came to do, only I did not expect to meet you, and when you started telling of Kore's father, I was so curious, I let you go on," Anna Lea paused expectantly.

"Of course, he may come in." Dahliah sat again, still pale from her fright. "Forgive me." She took out a scented handkerchief and held it to her nose to steady herself.

"Please come in, Justice," Kore, still wearing his baggy night shirt, winced as he pulled himself up to a sitting position. "I would come to you, but I am not dressed to receive company. It is rather early in the morning for all this fuss."

It was not proper for a lady to see his battle scars, but Anna Lea had heard from Martin that they were healing nicely but would still scar impressively, which was good news for Kore.

Justice turned slowly to meet Dahliah's eyes. She had recovered herself and nodded bravely. Moving into the room, Justice stood apart from the others.

It was strange to see him looking out of place. This was Justice, the King's Man, who could silence a room with a single glance.

"Will you tell us of Kore's father?" Anna Lea asked.

Dahliah glanced at Justice and nodded once more. "It is time it was told. Kore too needs to hear it. I thought by keeping it from him, I could protect him. I see now how wrong I was."

Kore did not protest.

"Kyler Eston was a bold, brave man. He was respected by everyone he met. Our home was often full of notable lords and ladies. It was a wonderful life we shared. I loved hosting and having our two sons exposed to so many great men and woman. The thought of them marrying well and having their own estates someday filled me with joy. Things began to change, but I would not admit it. Kyler started meeting with a group of men late at night. Their meetings were secret, and talk was hushed, so that even I could not overhear what was going on. When I asked about it, Kyler told me they were just good friends spending time together." Dahliah looked down at the handkerchief in her hands. "I knew it was not true, but I did not want the good times to end. So I turned a blind eye. I hosted more of the greats and prepared my sons to one day stand among them."

One night, as the men left, Kaden, my oldest, was with them. I begged his father not to take him. He was barely sixteen and had a life of success ahead of him. When I called after Kaden," she paused, as if frozen by the memory, "he turned his horse and looked at me. His eyes were filled with hatred, and I knew I would never see him again."

Kore reached out and put his hand on hers. "Mother, if it is too much, you need not go on."

She patted his hand and drew a shaky breath. "I have come this far, you must know, my son. You must understand why we left that life behind and came to live so close to the outskirts."

He took her hand in his and waited.

"Your father had been training Kaden in secret on how to use a sword and do all of the things I tried so hard to keep you from. That is why I would not allow you to own a sword, Kore. I lost two men to that piece of steel and could not bear to lose you too."

Justice shifted where he stood, and Dahliah looked up at him. "You were right in what you did, Justice. Kyler had become an evil man, plotting to do things I would have never thought possible of him." She looked across the room at the blank wall, remembering, "That night, they raided the estate of a wealthy family. The heir was killed by my own husband." Her eyes lifted to Anna Lea's, and a tear slid down her face.

Anna Lea stared at her, trying to take it all in. "My brother was killed in a night raid." She spoke slowly as the truth dawned on her. "It was Lord Eston who killed him."

"I am so sorry, Annalise," Dahliah was trying to stop her tears with the handkerchief.

Kore's voice took up the narrative, "My brother, Kaden, was also killed in the raid. Father was furious. He stormed and raged all day. No one could get near him. That night, very late, someone came to see my father. They met outside. I could see them in the moonlight but could not hear what was said."

Dahliah was sobbing now. Anna Lea rose and went to her. Sinking down beside the weeping lady, Anna Lea laid her head gently against Dahliah's knee. There were no words to comfort her.

Kore looked at Justice. "It was Wiley Oliver, wasn't it?" Justice, his eyes moist, nodded.

"My father commissioned him to kill Anna Lea's parents." The horror of it sunk in, and Kore's jaw muscles worked as he fought the emotion that welled up inside him.

Anna Lea bent forward, her face hidden in her hands. Her shoulders shook with silent sobs. Dahliah drew her up and they clung to one another, sharing the unbearable sorrow.

"That was years ago," Kore whispered, meeting Justice's eyes.

"Three years ago," Justice confirmed, letting the gravity of it sink in. He looked at Anna Lea. She had suffered in captivity for three, long years, pretending to be a simpleton in order to preserve her own life. Justice spoke again, "Her father and mother were murdered by an unknown man the night after her brother was killed. While she, left alive, was kidnapped and taken far from everything she knew and loved. It was not until a few months ago, long after Annalise Hillcrest was thought to be dead, that documentation had been found in the belongings of a recently deceased servant, revealing Wiley Oliver as the killer. Questions were asked, and the accusation was confirmed. It was then that I was sent by the king."

Kore thought of her terror when Milo was taking her away. She had been reliving that day, the day she lost everything. And it was Kore's family who had caused all of her pain.

Anna Lea, unaware of their gaze, was composing herself with deep shaky breaths. "Forgive me," She whispered, turning away to wipe her face with the corner of her long skirt.

Not knowing how else to help, Kore offered his mother

a corner of his sheet. Dahliah laughed a little and accepted.

Justice could see Kore in her laugh. Their eyes shared the same will to live.

"You do not have to go on, Mother," Kore told her sympathetically, having rubbed his own eyes dry with the back of his hand.

"We are a mess, aren't we?" Dahliah put her arm around Anna Lea who moved in close and leaned her head against her as a child would lean on her mother. "Can you bear the rest, my dear?" Dahliah asked Anna Lea.

Anna Lea nodded without lifting her head.

Taking a deep breath, Dahliah continued the story, "After the first raid on the Hillcrest estate, several of their servants fled to the king. They had seen Lord Eston kill Anna Lea's brother and went to plead for mercy and protection. The Hillcrest family was to follow once they had laid the boy to rest. Only they never had the chance. That night, the assassin hired by Lord Eston, killed Counselor and Lady Hillcrest. We feared you too had been killed, Annalise, but no trace of you could be found except a single bloodstained ribbon on the road." Dahliah paused, "Do you want to add anything?"

Anna Lea shook her head no, even after three years, the heartbreak of seeing her parent's killed was too painful to be spoken. She trembled with the memory of being dragged from her home, and felt the reassuring weight of Dahliah's arm around her.

"Justice came three days later. He approached your father, Kore, and read the judgment of the king. I will never forget the hardness in your father's face as he admitted to the murder. He believed so strongly that Hillcrest Estate's wealth should belong to him, that he had become hard as stone inside. I did not stay to see him killed. The servants helped me pack a few things, and I took Kore and fled. I fled the life and the guilt I knew I could never shake." She looked up at Justice, "Every day I feared that someday you would come for my son."

"You fled from the king's protection. He is just and would have helped you," Justice said softly.

"We lived in the shadow of the king, and it did my family no good."

Kore glanced at Justice, "It was not the king's fault, Mother. We lived in his realm, but we were not his subjects."

"Are we not born his subjects?" His mother looked confused, but Anna Lea smiled at him.

"That is a common misunderstanding. We are all born into his realm, but that alone does not make you his subject."

"Well spoken." Justice grinned at Kore, "I will leave you to explain it fully. Thank you, Lady Eston. That was hard for us all, but the truth brings freedom. It was an honor to meet you. Please know that you are always welcome in the presence of the king." Turning his attention to Anna Lea, Justice added, "We must start our journey. The king is expecting us."

The ladies rose, and Dahliah hugged Anna Lea tightly. "Be safe. I hope you can forgive me."

Anna Lea smiled and hugged her back. "All is forgiven, Lady Eston. You did me no wrong."

Dahliah held her at arm's length. Looking into Anna Lea's eyes, she said thoughtfully, "You, too, are a subject of the king."

"Yes, I am," Anna Lea agreed with a happy laugh. "I cannot wait to meet him."

Dahliah released her, and Anna Lea went to the bed where Kore sat propped in his night clothes. Kore seemed ashamed to meet her eyes.

"Goodbye, Kore," Anna Lea said bravely when he did not speak.

He looked up quickly as if afraid she would go without hearing what he wanted to say. "I am sorry for the pain my family has caused you. That I have caused you."

"I forgive you, Kore," Anna Lea answered, her face serious. "Truly I do. You did not take my family. Don't live in their shadow, Kore. You are a different man. You serve the king."

He nodded gratefully, biting his lip to keep back the emotions.

"Will the others travel with you?" Dahliah asked looking at Kore for help with their names.

"Martin and Sadie," Kore responded, wishing he were well enough to make the journey with them.

"Yes, they were packing the last of the supplies." Anna Lea looked guiltily at Justice. "We were to say our goodbyes and return to the horses, so they could come see you before we left."

Justice, with a glance at Dahliah for permission, went to the bedside and clasped Kore's hand firmly. "Get well quickly, my friend. The king has need of men like you."

Kore smiled, embarrassed and pleased by the praise from the King's Man. "For the king's honor."

Anna Lea and Justice replied together, "For the honor of the king!"

STRENGTH OF SILENCE

Eddie stayed where he was, listening. In the distance, a motor started up. He waited until it had faded before he stood. Dizziness washed over him, and he steadied himself against the counter. Still moving unsteadily, Eddie removed the floorboards and laid them aside. He heard something out front and froze. If the police caught him here, there would be no end of trouble. Moving toward the back door Eddie pushed it open. Outside, trash cans and a variety of other things littered the yard. A car motor rumbled toward him, and Eddie ran.

JASON ROPER TRILOGY

Infused with invincibility and trained for greatness, Jason Roper is set to fulfill his father's dreams. But when Roper deviates from the instructions he is given, he stumbles upon an expansive criminal network. Determined to use his power to help those in need, Jason Roper discovers that there are times when invincibility alone is not enough.

Is Jason Roper destined for greatness as he has been told, or is his life just a front for a larger, more sinister plan?

The Man Behind The Melody

The unexpected death of his twin sister threw Mark into a whirlwind of change. Disowned by his stepfather, Mark set out with only one goal in mind, to get as far away from the hateful man as possible. He clung desperately to the last link with his sister, her saxophone. Wandering the streets, Mark's path crossed with a stranger who could see potential no one else could see. Mark, an unwanted orphan, was offered the chance to become more than he had ever dreamed. But could the stranger be trusted?

Carbon
An Unforgettable Adventure

Carbon slipped out of bed and turned on the light. Taking a sheet of thick drawing paper from her desk she drew the face of the man the article simply called Roper. Pulling the picture she had drawn earlier from her file box, she laid them side by side on the desk. It was little or nothing to go on. The prisoner could have been a thousand different people. She had no face to compare. Suddenly the image of the stranger in the alley came to mind and Carbon frowned thoughtfully. He was the only one who would know.

Taken by the Deep

"Must be a storm." Jeremy tried to sound confident.

"It's not a storm, Jeremy." Lydia's face was white and her voice faded into a whisper. "Please, you've got to let me go."

They didn't seem to hear her. Their eyes were riveted on the swirling water before them. It rose slowly as if the waves were standing, then moved forward with hypnotic swiftness.

Lydia screamed as the waters dove toward them. The salty spray wrapped around her, wrenching her from their grasp and pulling her into its depth.

THE STRIKER OF CHOI

The health of the Striker is the health of Choi. If he goes hungry, the town of Choi will grow hungry. If he is injured, the townspeople will suffer injury. He must be protected at all costs and must never leave the town of his birth. If he were to leave, the curse of the town would be in the hands of strangers.

Striker knew the legend well, but was there more to the legend than he had been told?

In Visible Fear

Billy dropped back on the bed, flickering between the visible world and the invisible. His breathing was rapid and irregular.

"Keep quiet, Billy, and I'll do my best to keep them off your trail. They were asking about you today."

"Don't let them find me." Again, Billy grasped the man's shirt, terror in his eyes.

The dark man pried his fingers open and stepped away. "You keep your mouth shut, I'll do what I can."

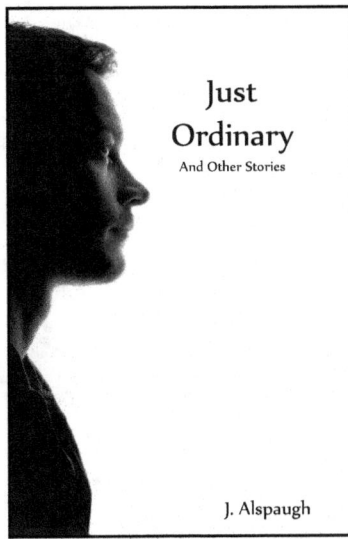

Just Ordinary
And Other Stories

Is there anyone who is truly just ordinary? Step into the world of fiction where heroes face mythical enemies, wrestle against enticing deceit, and battle fierce storms in a struggle for life. Experience heartbreak, adventure, and the ultimate sacrifice as you delve into the stories of *Just Ordinary*.

www.ingramcontent.com/pod-product-compliance
Lightning Source LLC
Chambersburg PA
CBHW061238170626
46809CB00007B/2729